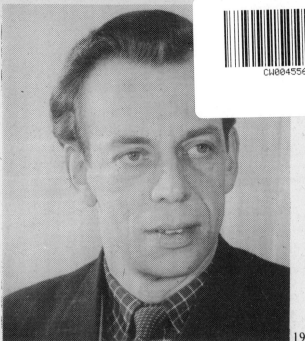

1956

JACK TREVOR STORY was born at Bengeo, Hertfordshire in 1917. He is the author of fifty three books. Amongst his best-known titles are *The Trouble with Harry, I Sit in Hanger Lane* and *Live Now, Pay Later*. He has written film scripts and TV scripts for series like *Public Eye, Budgie* and *No Hiding Place*. He has written scripts for Spike Milligan and for his own television series *You're Only Young Twice* (original title, *The Twilighters*). His films include *These Dangerous Years, Mix Me a Person* and *Live Now, Pay Later*. His articles and short stories have appeared in *Punch, The Listener, The Sunday Times, Men Only, Knave, The Times* and *The Guardian*, in which the weekly column chronicling his break-up with his girlfriend Maggie appeared (collected together in two books, *Letters to an Intimate Stranger* and *Jack on the Box*). These themes were worked into his recent television series, *Jack on the Box*, for ATV Television. Jack Trevor Story has been married twice and has had at least eight children. In 1977 he was awarded an Arts Council of Great Britain Creative Writing Fellowship. He now lives in Milton Keynes with his girlfriend Elaine.

LIVE NOW, PAY LATER is the third book in the Savoy Collected Editions of Jack Trevor Story's novels, and the first book in the famous Albert Argyle series. The other books are . . .

The Other Albert Argyle Books
Something for Nothing
The Urban District Lover

TV Tie-In
Jack on the Box

The Classic Novel Filmed by Alfred Hitchcock
The Trouble With Harry

And
Man Pinches Bottom
Screwrape Lettuce (Up River)
The Money Goes Round
One Last Mad Embrace
The Wind in the Snottygobble Tree

JACK TREVOR STORY

LIVE NOW, PAY LATER

SAVOY BOOKS
In association with
NEW ENGLISH LIBRARY
TIMES MIRROR

Copyright Jack Trevor Story
1963, 1980

Published by Savoy Books Ltd.,
279 Deansgate, Manchester M3 4EW,
England.

First published by
Secker & Warburg

Cover artwork: Harry Douthwaite

Typesetting: Arena Typesetting, Manchester

Printed by
S.E.T. Limited, Manchester

ISBN 0 86130 029 7

For Bill Johnson

Part One

JAM TODAY

1

ALBERT was late.

This was a feeling in his stomach rather than a matter of fact. There was nowhere he had to be this morning by any particular time; the tyranny of school had decided him into a career which made no demands of punctuality or personal convenience. He had purposely flopped the eleven-plus because he had heard that the local grammar school had a Saturday-morning attendance.

'There are two sorts of people in the world,' he used to tell his mother; 'slaves and masters.'

His mother, by the time he was fifteen, was already aware of this fact.

Now twenty-four and living in a bed-sitting-room, Albert was ironing yesterday's shirt by heating a table spoon in the gas-ring and rubbing it over his chest. Orphaned and alone, he had discovered most of the short cuts which make women unnecessary. He could cook a three-course meal on a gas ring in fifteen minutes flat, putting all the vegetables into one saucepan and sharing the flame with a frying-pan and then washing up in the potato water. The woman's confidence trick lay in creating a three-act drama out of their place in the kitchen.

'Feel my chin,' he would say to his girl-friends if he detected the possessive instinct. Then he would say: 'I have shaved for years in boiled-egg water without getting a single wart.' It always defeated them.

Albert struck two matches, blew them out, scraped off the carbon with his finger-nail and inserted the sticks into his collar slots. In selecting a tie to go with the continental-cut grey tweed suit Albert looked out of the window at the weather and decided it was probably spring; people were beginning to go to work without their coats. He whistled a passing girl and hailed her when she looked up at him; it was a pale, early-morning stranger's face, still inanimate and with the make-up predominating; but it lifted as she came alive a little and walked on, encouraged.

Albert smiled and selected the green-spotted bow tie, to the man who sold charm the early-morning whistle was the full extent of his early-morning exercises; everything was still working. He was big and blond and handsome and he had a way with him again today. He would do a lot of selling and a lot of collecting and somehow he would put back the ten pounds he had borrowed from the kitty.

The feeling of lateness came from being broke again. Like most men who dispense with authority and discipline and insist on being their own master, Albert's most pressing and urgent appointments were with himself. If you're broke, you're late; if you've been slacking, you're late; the self-employed man is either asleep or running.

Albert was not entirely self-employed — though this would be news to Mr Callendar, his boss; his card, gold-embossed, would prove that he was senior sales representative for Callendar's Warehouse who sold everything from vacuum cleaners to shoes, cocktail cabinets to transistor radios on a weekly door-to-door basis. He earned twelve pounds a week basic, plus commission on all he sold. And he spent rather more than this, whatever it was; thirty or forty pounds he could accurately predict and overspend.

'The most important thing if you want to be a success,' he used to tell his mother, 'is to keep up appearances.'

His mother, dragging herself off to work with her varicose veins and ulcer, was too tired to argue the point.

Ready now, Albert had a quick think for things forgotten. It was Wednesday, a neither here nor there day. He opened the flap of a cocktail cabinet and wardrobe combined — a strong Callendar line in a bed-sitter community. With a six-inch rule he measured the level of whisky in one bottle and gin in another, noting the figures on a card and initialling them with the date. This one solitary attention to a meticulous economy started him off into the day with the feeling that he was a methodical man. The man who doesn't know where forty pounds a week goes can live with himself if he knows definitely where five shillings of it goes.

And in fact the reason Albert had chosen the spirits to be meticulous about was that for one thing it was easy to do, once he had remembered it, and for another he didn't like people like Jeff and Arnold drinking his spirits for nothing and not replacing. Considering that he was doing them a favour by letting them bring birds in; they paid him for it, but it was still an inconvenience. More than once he had had to stand out in the rain while one of them finished, and there was always the risk that it would get talked about and he would lose the room.

In the beginning it was agreed between the three of them that they would stick to vintage cider which was getting almost one hundred per cent results back in nineteen fifty-eight and fifty-nine; but either the girls had become immunized to the apple or else they had got wise to it and now straight scotch or gin-and-tonic was the usual request. And some of the girls Jeff and Arnold found weren't worth either.

Albert clattered down the stairs and across the second-floor landing feeling like a polished diamond in a pig-iron setting. In the the big old Victorian house the bed-sitting-rooms were kept according to their occupants' tastes, but the stairs and passages were a no-man's-land of bare boards, peeling wallpaper, and brown paint; nobody's responsibility.

Through a partly-open door he saw a black man shaving.

'Mon'n baas!' Albert called.

'Hi, white man!' came the reply.

Albert ran on down to the ground floor, feeling pleased; he had never seen the Negro before, yet his cheerful crack had been accepted in the right spirit. There was a secret in getting on with people, with strangers, and

Albert felt that he knew it. It was a skilled business, a stock-in-trade. He would never starve; if you could sell yourself you could sell anything. He lost no opportunity in giving people gratuitous samples of himself and thus reinforcing his ego and his belief in himself.

Checking himself, checking the effects he had upon people, checking their reactions to what he was selling — the smile, the word, the package — was a continuous process with Albert. As he often looked into a mirror to rehearse his smile, a new wry or waggish facial expression or a new wisecrack, so he looked often at his personality as reflected in other people's reactions.

His ability to manipulate people gave him a sense of power — the first essential in salesmanship. Or acting, or statesmanship, come to that. He also felt that he had all the other essentials; charm, honesty, humility, sincerity. Sincerity above all. Sincerity really paid off; with selling, with girls, with getting out of a scrape.

With the equipment, physical and mental, that Albert now had he felt like a master puppeteer; for instance, housewives' psychology he had down to a fine art. In the affluent society of today the tally-boy was the new messiah, bible-punching the full-colour brochures which carried the cleansing needs of humanity. You get automatic temperature control, you get automatic time control, you get double penetration supersonic washrays. . . . Everybody was getting and the tally-boy was giving.

Albert was sufficiently cynical to know all this and sufficiently susceptible to believe it. He was trapped in hire-purchase debt as deeply as any of his customers. He would refuse to admit that this was a weakness — it was yet another facet of his techniques. If you sell on easy terms you've got to live on easy terms: otherwise where's your sincerity? Where's your consumer identification? This he had explained to Mr Callendar the last time he had been caught raising a personal loan out of his takings to avert a judgement summons.

'Git the goods in the 'ouse, boy,' Mr Callendar had told him. 'That's all you have to do — this stuff sells itself.'

No wonder Albert despised his boss for his crude, unsubtle, unappreciative approach to the applied science of selling. But Albert felt that he also had power over Mr Callendar; if he left tomorrow and took his clients to another firm — or started up on his own, given the capital — he could put Callendar's Warehouse out of business.

Unknown to Albert Mr Callendar knew this and did not lose any sleep. Albert was a good tally-boy because he was like every other tally-boy; and Mr Callendar knew tally-boys. You give them a small basic wage, a Mini-Minor van, easy hours, and a lot of rope. You allow them ten per cent commission on sales and another ten per cent fiddle on sales and expenses and you give them the sack or send them to prison when they go over this mark. Or you wait for them to get their sales up so high they ask for a partnership, then sack them.

Albert was the most brilliant door-to-door salesman Mr Callendar had ever had; this meant, by the same token, that he was a super show-off, a super-womanizer, a super-fiddler and confidence trickster — the last man to have in any business except as a tally-boy.

Unknown to Albert, all the power that he thought he had and all the power the other tally-boys thought they° had was harnessed to Mr Callendar and his simple creed of gitting the goods in the 'ouse. Tally-boys to Mr Callendar were just a means of getting the goods in the house. They were a necessary evil in the distribution of consumer goods. Tally-boys had no power of any kind because they had no money. Nobody with money would become a tally-boy. Nobody with any self-respect would become a tally-boy. No man with an ounce of real ability or even with any ordinary sensibility or human feeling could stand on a doorstep in his best suit and pretend that he was doing working people a favour.

The good tally-boy was the man who enjoyed the smart suit and the van and a pocketful of other people's money, the handling of new shiny goods and the vicarious pleasure — not always vicarious — of chatting up other men's wives while the children were at school. The good tally-boy possessed elements of delinquency, amorality and furtive adventure; showmanship, self-delusion, and self-aggrandizement. The good tally-boy was perennially and incurably improvident; when he bullied a woman for her arrears he really needed the money.

Mr Callendar therefore had the greatest respect for Albert as a tally-boy — and would never allow him within miles of an executive position in the firm. He knew by Albert's increasing sales and growing arrogance that such an application was nearly due, but happily he did not even have to waste time considering it. Albert was a brilliant salesman but he could go tomorrow. What Albert didn't know, and what few salesmen knew, was that it was not the selling that made a business, but the buying. The executive brains of any business was in the buying. A bad salesman could lose you profits, but a bad buyer could bankrupt you.

Mr Callendar did his own buying. He bought wisely and well from those companies who backed every selling campaign and every new domestic appliance with a million pounds' worth of advertising. He bought the goods which were already sold by a system of mass-hypnosis through the mediums of television, newspapers, periodicals, films, and direct-mail. He dealt, not with that section of the buying public who sleep-walked their way into the shops as willing victims, but with those equally hypnotized people who were waiting to have the goods thrust into their homes. The tally-boy had no real selling to do, it had already been accomplished; his job was to insinuate the merchandise across the doorstep as painlessly as possible with no mention of money. Then, calling a week later when the customer had had time to become irrevocably addicted to spin drying or stereophonic sound, he started collecting the small, unmissable tally.

The good tally-boy, in the name of a higher standard of living, could trap half a family's income every week.

Jack Trevor Story

If there was any difficulty in collecting the money, the good tally-boy could bully and threaten the length of a garden path and bring out the neighbours — the most effective system of blackmail; or if that failed he was backed, because of the agreement which no hypnotized person remembered signing, with all the terrifying paraphernalia of the law from solicitors' letters to county court summonses and even prison. The good tally-boy, in Mr Callendar's opinion, was a low but essential form of life and Albert was the best tally-boy he had ever had.

Albert, starting his day and checking his charm and his power, was totally unaware of this view of himself — and his brother tally-boys Jeff and Arnold — held by their boss. If he had any knowledge of any part of the truth about himself and his job he successfully submerged it in the remotest regions of his subconscious. He was cynical about the people he trapped into high living on easy terms but was ignorant and blind to the fact that he was equally trapped by the same glossy snares. To keep up appearances, Albert was in debt up to his ears.

Besides such small things as electric razors, transistor radios, tape recorders, typewriters, radiograms, suits, shirts, coats and shoes, there was a car which he was now running and another which had been reclaimed by the HP company but on which he still had a two-hundred pound liability. Had Albert kept up all his payments — an impossibility since he no longer knew what they were — his total weekly outgoings of easy payments would have totalled twenty-two pounds a week; ten pounds a week more than his basic wage.

And on top of all this, after two years he still owed ten pounds for his mother's funeral.

Albert was very late indeed and it was getting later.

2

CALLENDAR'S Warehouse was a shabby double-fronted shop with its windows partly painted out and partly smashed in. It stood in a smoke-blackened street of terraced houses and small shops opposite a large, grim prison-like building which had once been a cardboard box factory. This was one of the few remaining depressed areas due for eventual demolition and development; a criss-cross of ugly streets lying between the modern, sodium-lighted shopping centre and the main railway line to the north. There were old, disused factories, empty blocks of Victorian offices, silent workshops, and sprawling yards behind high rotting gates, crowded with builders' supplies.

From Victorian years up to the late nineteen-thirties the area had constituted the busy heart of a town once devoted to and famed for its gay straw hats and frou frou millinery. A long history in ribbon and felt, boxes and blocks, steam presses and lace was written on the gravestones of green brass door plates and isinglass lettering on black-screened windows. Callendar's Warehouse stood like a traitor in the graveyard, dispensing the mass-produced luxuries which had put the fine arts out of business.

Callendar's shop window had been smashed by an angry girl who had thrown a bicycle through it. It was now boarded up and the timber slats bore the commemorative legend in white chalk:

TREASURE WAS HERE

A reminder obscure to the passers-by but clear, indelible, and painful to Albert Argyle, who knew what it meant.

Jeff and Arnold were in the showroom selecting wares

for the day and at the same time listening to Mr Callendar who stood at the counter chatting up a new customer. The young woman, pretty, nicely-shaped, was plainly ill at ease and had not yet been indoctrinated into credit buying. The state of strain which resulted from this was composed of many subtle elements. Many contributory facts of which they were all aware, but which could not be allowed to emerge baldly. She wanted some things and she hadn't the money to pay them. She couldn't admit this outright. If she had had the money she would not have come to Callendar's at all but would have gone to one of the many shops in the town which offered a wider choice and lower prices. Mr Callendar couldn't admit this. She had been recommended to Callendar's by a similarly hard-up friend who consistently defaulted on her payments. Neither of them could mention this.

'I heard your stuff was very good,' Coral Wentworth was saying.

'The best, madam,' Mr Callendar assured her. 'We only have the best. You pay a little more for quality and it's worth it in the long run. . . . '

Coral began to relax; Marjorie was right, it was quite a nice firm to deal with once you got inside. Mr Callendar began to relax; he fully appreciated that the few customers who began by visiting his blind-fronted shop looked both ways before entering. Credit buying was the accepted thing these days, but so was prompt treatment for venereal disease and nobody liked to be seen going in.

'I'd like to see some children's clothing,' Coral told him. 'School blazers, trousers, dresses, and so forth — some shoes.'

'Yes, of course — you can't afford inferior quality there. The youngsters go through clothes like a tank, these days — of course you realize,' Mr Callendar added, apologetically, 'we don't deal in cash, here, Mrs Wentworth — you don't object to weekly payments, do you? The usual shilling in the pound — most people do it these days and it's not missed. You can have twenty pounds worth of stuff for one pound a week — after all, who wants to save up for things these days? By the time you get it you may not be here with things as they are — and incidentally if anybody drops an atom bomb before you've finished paying we automatically cancel the account.'

'I see,' Coral said. Then, at the look of strain on Mr Callendar's face, she realized that he had made a joke. She laughed. 'Oh yes, I see!'

Mr Callendar laughed also and so did Jeff and Arnold and Hetty behind the cash desk who, until now, had kept a discreet silence and made an elaborate pretence of not noticing there was a customer in the shop.

Now that the ice was broken, Mr Callendar was happy to include his staff in the transaction. It was not really a counter trade, most of their customers were prepared to shop from catalogues or samples taken to their door; but the few who came to the warehouse he liked to attend to himself and try to preserve some kind of normality.

The door-to-door salesman had a technique unsuited to counter service. It was not that he wasn't at home in a shop, he was at home anywhere — that was the trouble. The tally-boy technique was essentially theatrical and familiar; it was related to the technique of the variety uncle, the quiz-master, the phoney let's-get-together man. 'Good morning, darling, I've brought you some black undies that'll drive your husband raving mad,' was often acceptable in the intimacy of the home between a tally-boy and an otherwise bored housewife, but over the counter with other people present it could lose customers.

Women like Mrs Wentworth had to be inaugurated into the system and Mr Callendar was happy to get the process over and done with. He didn't like the selling side of his business; he preferred the buying and the book-keeping. The tally-boys who sold on easy terms and the people who bought on easy terms he thoroughly despised, even though they made him rich.

'Besides getting the best goods money can buy,' Mr Callendar went on, 'you'll have the added pleasure of one of our charming young men calling on you every week.'

He introduced Mr Jefferies, an ageing tally-boy who looked and acted like the old Zube caricature of the villain Jasper Gadd whose throat just like his heart was bad. A polished, bald dome of a head, a fair moustache, and a long chin which dropped in a smirk as his hooded eyes possessed Mrs Wentworth for a moment with a calculating passion which had sold a hundred washing machines.

'Charmed,' he murmured, wrinkling his nose.

And Arnold, Mr Baxter, a large, rubicund, countrified young man with a big, honest, ingenuous grin and an apparently simple mind who said 'Pleased to meet you' shyly enough, but whom Mr Callendar knew to be as crudely sexed as a stud bull once the gate was opened. Arnold, a recently joined trainee, was taking the place of Max who had gone to prison after getting into a tight spot and trying to get out of it by holding a private auction of three hundred pounds' worth of Callendar's domestic appliances in a disused church hall. Arnold was not likely to get into that kind of trouble; indeed he was not obvious tally-boy material at all except to someone who knew the type as thoroughly as did Mr Callendar. He had come in for the interview clean, smart, and bringing a refreshing air of dairy herds and green pastures. He couldn't talk, his thinking was slow, he knew nothing about their wares, he seemed shy of strangers and Mr Callendar was about to dismiss him when he noticed Arnold absently picking his nose.

From this Mr Callendar had reasoned there was more to Arnold than appeared on the surface; men who picked their nose in public were often underprivileged in some ghastly, unwholesome way. Later his faith was justified when he had learned that Arnold had once worked for a shady second-hand car dealer who had been handling stolen cars when the police caught up with him; it was to Arnold's immense credit, in Mr Callendar's opinion, that the car dealer and all his staff had gone to prison with the single exception of Arnold, against whom, apparently, there had been no evidence. Or at least, no believable evidence in the face of Arnold's steadfast denials.

Nobody could look at Arnold and say 'Guilty'; this was Arnold's personal gimmick and but for that one obnoxious personal habit, he could have fooled even Mr Callendar.

Arnold was already proving his worth in the territory carefully selected for him which covered, since Mr Callendar knew more about consumer identification than Albert would have given him credit for, those far-flung red brick slums, the council-house estates, which festered on the once green hills outside the town. He understood the problems of the new-rich working classes and spoke their lauguage fluently, since he also had graduated from one of their glacial secondary-modern palaces; he also wrote their language in his occasional sales memos to Mr Callendar:

Somefink up the spout on Mrs Fishers washing machine can we service same soon as poss? Customer flaming. Second time in a month, init? Can we send bod up there instead of hafting to hump machine down here?
Signed: A. Baxter — Junior Sales Rep.

Of course, Arnold would never do for the residential districts of the town. The middle and upper class territories were covered by Jeff and Albert; at least, that was the theory. In practice, as Mr Callendar well knew, the tally-boys swapped clients between themselves as if the housewives were slave girls — not that any of them suspected what went on. Jeff would give Albert two blondes for one redhead, even if it meant making a three-mile journey out of his territory. There were other and finer considerations in their bartering; whether the customers were 'easy' or not came into it, if they were prompt with payment; whether they were married, single, widowed or divorced, twenty-five or forty.

One of the many chaotic results of such a haphazard exchange of accounts from one muddled book to another muddled book was that none of the tally-boys knew exactly where he stood financially and neither did the firm. There were machines and clothing going out in vast quantities and money coming in and it was Hetty's job to give the accounts some semblance of sanity and balance. In order to do this she had long ago discarded all the garbled explanations from the three tally-boys and resorted to equating stock and money by a simple algebraic system all her own which bore no resemblance to the facts but gave a healthy end column.

'We'll say that Mrs Granger has paid for the vacuum cleaner but not for the refrigerator, then when Mrs Bockett clears her spin dryer we can put that as clearing Mrs Granger's refrigerator — and vice-versa,' Hetty would tell Jeff on a Friday night, which, again theoretically, was supposed to be the night for tally statements.

'That's all right,' Jeff would say, 'except that Mrs Granger hasn't got that refrigerator — if you remember I swapped it for a radiogram with Albert.'

'I thought he still owed you a washing machine — remember that demonstration model? Or did that come in?'

'No, we wrote that off — it burst into flames, remember? Albert owes Arnold three transistor radios off his dem stock — '

'Oh, leave it to me!' Hetty would say, and get busy with a rubber and pencil; she found it necessary to keep the accounts in pencil up until auditing time, then after final adjustments she would ink them over. Hetty was a plump, blonde, placid, happy-go-lucky mum of fifty who didn't give a damn about the job beyond keeping the books 'tidy' as she called it. To this end she had taken care of serious deficits by inventing temporary arrears, and large incomprehensible surpluses by inventing new clients complete with addresses and account numbers. Some she copied from gravestones.

'Well, it seems to work,' she would tell her family when recounting the day's activities. 'Nobody's said nothing.'

After three years of Hetty's book-keeping nobody short of Einstein himself could possibly have made any coherent remark about the Callendar's Warehouse accounts. Mr Callendar, who knew more about tally selling than Einstein, made perfect sense of it; he knew that complete disorder of the tally-boys' kind needed complete disorder of Hetty's kind to produce something that was approximately order. While pretending to keep his eye on the daily transactions and weekly accounts he in fact concentrated only on the major situation of money in, money out, and stock.

The overall unsoundness of the people who lived on a hire-purchase economy of jam today and the dubiety and furtiveness of the tally-boys who gave it to them was reflected on a larger scale right through the business. With every credit squeeze or raising of the bank rate Mr Callendar creamed off his capital and profits to a Swiss bank; with each lightening of the situation he creamed it back. And ever since the possibility that Britain might join the European Common Market Mr Callendar had kept a case ready packed in anticipation of the kind of calamitous national prosperity which would demand higher quality and competitive prices for exportable goods, wages in accordance with work done — regardless of tea breaks — and unemployment for those who disliked hard work — regardless of their hire-purchase commitments.

Such a state of affairs could leave Callendar's Warehouse with a load of bad debts, a pile of frozen stock and the prospect of those smaller manufacturers who were geared to small-quantity shoddy production for the home market either closing down or frantically calling in all credit. The dark possibility of a population living according to its means on an orderly cash basis was terrifying to Mr Callendar and he had made his plans to get out.

His pretence of being *au fait* at all times with the trivial everyday tangle of the business was necessary in order to keep his staff on their toes. Tally-boys were vulnerable through their sheer inefficiency; Mr Callendar had only to be specifically critical from time to time to create the impression that he knew everything that was going on — a horrifying thought for Albert, Arnold, and Jeff.

'These expenses,' he would say to Albert. 'They're two pounds five over the top — you're forty miles up on your mileage meter, you've charged three lunches too many, and you've duplicated stationery and printing expenses. Watch it, will you?'

Albert would watch it for weeks after that and so would the others, even though the whole list had come straight out of Mr Callendar's imagination. Since expenses also came out of the tally-boy's imagination there was no core of hard fact to fight criticism.

With Hetty's book-keeping, Mr Callendar would interfere only when it was glaringly necessary.

'These infra-red cookers, Hetty — where did you get 'em? They haven't been put on the market yet — and you've got three sold and one coming back for repair.'

'Sorry, Mr Callendar — I must have seen it in a magazine or on the telly. Sorry, Mr Callendar I'm sure.'

'That's all right, Hetty, love. You'd better change it to Crosby's Mark Four cooker — then the prices might come out about right.'

'All right then.' Hetty would scan her books with an appearance of high efficiency, then add: 'Or should I make it Mark Two? We've got ever such a lot of them. . .'

And she would get busy with pencil and rubber and make it tidy; it was like doing an immensely complicated jig-saw puzzle in which the picture didn't matter as long as the pieces roughly fitted together.

Coral Wentworth, opening her first account with Callendar's was, of course, unaware of all this, but she could detect that it was not any ordinary shop. Marjorie had hinted as much when she told her about the tussle she had had with the young man who called for the payments; she had not said how she got into the fight nor how she came out of it but she hadn't appeared to be complaining. It was just one of Marjorie's amusing anecdotes. Lately, when Coral had grown envious of all the marvellous clothes and furnishings Marjorie seemed able to afford on the weekly payment system and had inquired about Callendar's she had become quite reticent; almost as though she didn't want Coral to be in on it. Or else — and Coral had heard it was true up and down the street — Marjorie had got into difficulties with the payments and didn't want her name mentioned.

'It's fifteen Cavendish Street, is it?' Mr Callendar was saying now. He produced a printed form. 'Just a formality, Mrs Wentworth — all you need do is sign it.' His tone said he wanted to make everything easy for her, rather than: 'For God's sake don't read it.'

To cover the moment as she signed he made a little friendly conversation. They had several good customers in Cavendish Street — was it Mrs Mason the schoolteacher's wife who recommended her there? And at her hesitation he added that Mrs Mason was one of their best and most valued customers, making no mention of the odd state of her account and the fight the tally-boys had had for the privilege of calling on her. Marjorie Mason was a dish, apparently.

"Well yes, it was,' Coral admitted now.

Mr Callendar looked regretfully across the shop at his tally-boys who were still busy selecting their goods for the day. 'Sorry, boys — I'm afraid this is Mr Argyle's territory —'

'Would that be Albert?' Coral asked, adding, at the little man's fleeting anxiety: 'I believe that's what Marjorie calls him.'

'That's Albert — he's very popular with the ladies. Charming, of course, a real gentleman, never a word out of place.'

Coral smiled her pleasure; but that isn't what Marjorie said about him; not that she didn't want you to think every man went wild about her, because she did; it wasn't difficult to guess who made the first overtures, no man attacked you without a little encouragement; and it was hard to see how she had surrounded herself with so many beautiful things on a schoolteacher's salary; although Cedric had to do several part-time jobs to keep up with her; or was it just to keep him out of the way?

'Mr Jefferies . . .' Mr Callendar had noticed Jeff's sulky reaction to the news that she was going to be in Albert's book instead of his and offered his consolation. 'Take Mrs Wentworth up to Boy's Wear to start with, will you?'

'Lovely!' Jeff said, extending his arm in a corny old-world gesture and moving towards the stairs.

Mr Callendar inwardly groaned; no shop assistant did or said things like that. He added to the new customer as a by-the-way: 'Does your husband work locally, Mrs Wentworth?'

'Yes, he's a foreman at the tractor works — he doesn't have to sign, does he?'

Mr Callendar shook his head and smiled his satisfaction; she was trying to make the housekeeping stretch a little farther without her husband knowing; the best kind of customer. He called Jeff back and muttered: 'Take her through electrical goods.'

When Albert breezed into the shop half an hour later Mrs Wentworth was stooping behind the counter with Jeff looking at children's shoes.

'Ah, Albert!' Mr Callendar exclaimed, realizing a little too late that Albert would start the day as always with a rehearsal of his doorstep wit. 'I've got a new client for you — '

'And I have something for you, Mr Callendar — a new domestic appliance!' He could have been on a stage, rubbing his hands and sharing the patter between Callendar, Arnold, and Hetty. 'Economical, labour-saving, well-styled — it's called a wife!'

Mr Callendar laughed, swiftly, but Albert went for the payoff.

'Simple to operate, few moving parts — you simply screw it on the bed and it does the housework!'

There was a moment's silence, but only the time Hetty

took to work it out. In the silence, keeping below counter level, Mrs Wentworth met Jeff's probing eyes.

'I think these will do,' she said, with a dry throat.

'Good, good,' Mr Callendar shouted, slightly demented.

Albert now saw the customer and fell silent.

It was then that Hetty roared with vulgar laughter. 'That's a good one! Oh dear, oh dear! I must tell my old man that one!' She looked at Mrs Wentworth with streaming eyes. 'Did you hear that one?'

Mr Callendar hurried to the office: 'You must excuse me, madam — I have to go. I leave you in good hands — business meeting . . .'

The young woman watched the little man hurry out of the shop clutching a bag of golf clubs.

'Social climber,' Albert explained, smiling at his new customer, and regaining his good spirits and his confidence. 'There are no heights these days, you know — you climb sideways along the golf course!'

Coral Wentworth laughed with the others. Getting rid of Mr Callendar was like getting rid of the sober guests at the drunken party. Inhibition, never heavier than gossamer in this establishment, had blown away.

'Well, introduce me, Jeff,' Albert demanded. And in a theatrical aside to Arnold: 'Another of your washing machines is coming in, Arnold — do me a favour, don't sell washing machines to people who want to keep their coal in them — sell 'em refrigerators, there's no moving parts!'

Hetty was smiling proudly at the customer: 'He's a real card!'

Outside Mr Callendar sat for a moment in his car, knowing that everything would be all right now that he wasn't there; they were really all of a kind. He looked across the street at the empty windows of the old box factory and his spirits lightened. A broad white-painted wooden arrow had been erected all around the building to bracket it from the others; a big notice bore the announcement of this valuable commercial site for sale under the banner of Chas. Arthur Ltd, auctioneers and estate agents.

Mr Callendar had vaguely formed and nebulously held ambitions about that site. If the government didn't sabotage the credit business and if he didn't crash, then the chances were he would be able to interest enough local capital to demolish and build on the box-factory site; it would be nice to have a real retail business with real shop assistants and a valuable office block above as a property investment.

When Mr Callendar said he was going to a business meeting he was telling the truth. The kind of men who could afford the time to play golf during the working week were the kind of men who could raise capital; they were sometimes also the kind of men who could afford time out for influential things like local government and the magisterial benches. Mr Callendar's target for today was a certain Reginald Corby who happened to be a junior partner in the estate agents firm of Chas. Arthur; although Corby had no financial resources as yet — something that made him that more manipulatable — he did have the building site in his pocket and as a strong member of the Labour Party and club he was also angling for a place on the local council. And Mr Callendar was an expert in the art of wooing with a bad game of golf.

Mr Callendar's inner image of the new Callendar Building, all glass and satin-walnut, was rudely shattered by the sound of Hetty's loud cackle of laughter coming from the showroom; the palace of the future vanished and he was jerked back to the necessary now and present. Mr Callendar started his motor and drove away, as though trying to escape.

They were a vulgar lot; Hetty, the tally-boys, everybody in the business. No doubt when she was sufficiently warmed up the shy Mrs Wentworth would soon be regaled with their favourite record on the tape recorder. He had come in one day to find the three tally-boys — it had been in Max's day, and even worse — having what they called a farting contest in the textile department, putting the vile and noisy triumphs on magnetic tape. Max's last gesture before the police came for him was to substitute the tape on the demonstration model in the showroom and Mr Callendar, demonstrating to a new customer, had been subjected to the most embarrassing experience of his life.

Mr Callendar had outgrown those kind of people and this kind of business. He was a common man and he knew it; he had more than once overheard Albert mimicking the 'Git the goods in the 'ouse' slogan. But you could rise above a lack of education and your environment — if you had money. It was already becoming less of a strain to remember his aitches and to modulate his voice in the company of decent people. And it might be a good idea to change his Cresta for a second-hand Bentley like Corby's — he swerved and braked sharply as a lorry came out of a side turning.

'Cunt!' Mr Callendar screamed.

3

'I THINK I'll have one of those white nylon-fur fireside rugs,' Coral Wentworth was saying. 'Marjorie's got one of those, hasn't she?'

'And she uses it,' Jeff said, smirking. 'I know it well!'

Albert ignored him and said: 'Oh, you know Mrs Mason?'

'We all know Mrs Mason, don't we?' Jeff put in.

'She's rather sweet,' Coral said. 'In her way.'

Jeff clicked his tongue and said: 'Any time!'

'All right, Jeff — stop kidding and don't insult the customers,' Albert told him. Jeff hadn't the wit or the halfwit to know that if you spoke like that about one customer then it would be taken for granted that you were the same about all of them; it was not the best way to encourage a relationship.

Coral had already appreciated this point and her feelings were towards Albert. 'I thought *you* called on Mrs Mason?'

'She's changed hands four times since she was first registered,' Jeff said.

Arnold, who had been listening with bull-red face and watering eyes, said: 'Is that the one Max measured for jeans when she was wearing a shortie nightie?'

Hetty cackled her delight and looked at the new customer: 'They're a lot of sex maniacs, you know!'

'You speak for yourself,' Albert said. 'I think you're all going a bit too far — especially in front of a customer. I'm sorry about this,' he said, sincerely, to Mrs Wentworth. 'Can I show you anything else?'

'Famous last words,' Jeff said. But at the look on Albert's face he drifted away to sort over his own stock.

'What does it all come to?' Coral asked. She was suddenly apprehensive at the mounting pile of goods on the counter. She laughed, ruefully: 'This place is like an Aladdin's cave.'

'Mind what you rub, madam,' Jeff called across.

'Come into the office and we'll tot it up,' Albert told her.

They went into the office, leaving Jeff, Arnold and Hetty sniggering together.

'What an awful man!' Coral exclaimed, softly.

Albert registered his own disgust. 'They're like dirty-minded school kids, some of them . . . '

Their mutual disgust drew them together; there was a silent communion of common feeling as Albert totted up the cost of the goods. Coral liked Albert very much and had completely forgotten his opening joke; a tribute to his technique and it explained why he was senior salesman.

'Thirty-three pounds seven and ninepence — we'll knock off the odd shillings and pence, shall we?'

'Thank you — but it's more than I intended spending, to tell you the truth.'

'It's only thirty-three bob a week — say it quickly,' Albert said.

'How much does Marjorie — Mrs Mason — pay a week?

Or shouldn't I ask?'

'You shouldn't, but I'll tell you . . . ' Albert put his arm around her shoulders and whispered, his face in her hair: 'Five pounds a week — when she pays it!'

Coral's thoughts were racing; it was probably true what she had heard and suspected. 'However does she do it?'

Albert met her eyes, man to woman. 'Oh, you know — it's a bit of a struggle sometimes . . . '

Coral suppressed a smile, but let him know that she appreciated the joke; it was quite different with just the two of them, in private.

'Well,' she said, 'if she can do it, I can do it.'

'Eh!' Albert said, waggishly.

They laughed together. It was the beginning of a weekly relationship which could last longer than a marriage.

Mrs Wentworth was in Callendar's Warehouse something less than an hour, but in that time she had been subjected to the full tally treatment — the familiarity, the vulgarity, the intimacy, the nudging lifyness, the sheer filth, veiled and unveiled, the inauguration, the indoctrination — so that on leaving she experienced a sense of shock when Albert said decorously:

'Good morning, madam.'

'Good morning,' she said, blushing — half-betrayed as though at sudden coldness from a lover, half-embarrassed because she had in a curious involuntary way gone along with the familiarities and was therefore rebuked, half — for there were more than two halves to her mixed feelings — stunned at the things which had been said; half frightened at the amount of housekeeping money she had mortgaged — also involuntarily — on things which were not really essential and which she had not set out to buy. And then she stopped in the doorway, she had forgotten the most important item — Timothy's pants and vests. But she couldn't go back now.

Jeff was peering over the painted window, watching her rear as she walked away. He turned back to Albert: 'Talking of moving parts — how about transferring her to my account? I'll give you fourteen Devon Road for her?' Albert was not interested. Jeff quickly thumbed through his book: 'Eighty-four Hillary Crescent? She's a widow — you can spend nights there. You know I can never spend nights out.'

'Do you mind?' Albert said. 'I like to get finished by six too you know — besides, I can't stand women who only operate after dark. Anyway, I've broken the ice there — I'm sticking.'

'The breakfulness and the stickingfulness, if I may say so, old chappie, is terrific — as Hurree Jamset Ram Singh might put it — what!' Jeff laughed at Albert's lack of response. 'But there, you wouldn't know about that — no education!'

Jeff Jefferies's education had come almost entirely from the *Magnet* and the *Gem* of the thirties; in common with many of his contemporaries who went from elementary schools to errand-boy jobs he had assimilated an entire public school world complete with majors and minors, shells, removes and upper fifths, tuck shops, boot boys, heads and matrons, halves and hols, prep and rugger. It had shaped his attitude, his choice of friends, his vocabulary, his diction, his facial expressions, and the way he held his head. His ties and scarves, obscurely striped, obscurely coloured, never quite challengeable, had their origins in the misty ancient piles of Greyfriars, St Franks, and St Jims while the only boyhood friends he cared to remember were Harry Wharton, Bob Cherry, D'Arcy, Ram Singh, the only enemies those rotters in the sixth. This not discreditable veneer was, however, only eggshell thick and lacked the strengthening qualities of the real thing of creed and code, heredity and tradition; Jeff Jefferies — the yolk, that is — remained a soft gooey amalgam of errand-boy smut and workaday vulgarity; the fictitious boy had never matured into a fictitious man. Jeff had grown slowly and naturally, dirty joke by sexual malpractice, into the tally-boy slot; he could still quote in dog Latin, still maintain a 'varsity accent, but he could also speak freely of what he did to his wife and where he had suddenly discovered spots.

Albert didn't like Jeff Jefferies. They were different. They were both tally-boys, they were motivated and activated by the same desires, the same urges and the same shapes — it was the only thing that would keep a tally-boy busy — yet with Albert it was different. Albert could fall in love several times a week, twice in a day; but Jeff Jefferies didn't know what it was. On the inter-polated line between masculine and feminine, Jeff Jefferies was masculine; he had no woman in him; he had never felt the thrill of a touch of hands or a gaze of eyes, never sensed the woman's need for tenderness or fulfil-ment or protection. Love as he understood it was soppy, un-English and embarrassing — as any decent, full-blooded, rugger-playing boy knew. Jeff Jefferies could cut into one of Albert's many soliloquies about a pretty girl he had seen walking in the sun with: 'But did you get there old chappy, that's the point!'

But it wasn't the point and there was the difference between them.

'Tell you what. Tell you what I'll do,' Jeff persisted, following Albert, who was now parcelling up Mrs Went-worth's purchases and stacking them on the shelves for eventual delivery. 'I'll part exchange you Mrs O'Connell and that spin dryer I've got that needs a bit of attention — Hetty's cleared it as paid on the books.'

'No thanks — forget it, will you?'

'How about the girls in the basement flat behind the technical school — there's five of them, all students.'

'I've finished with single girls who don't know how to take care of themselves,' Albert said.

Jeff laughed and looked across at Hetty and Arnold, who was now trying to make an old vacuum cleaner work. 'Now we're back to Treasure again,' he said.

Albert stopped what he was doing and glared at Jeff. 'Don't talk about Treasure, if you don't mind.'

'Who's Treasure?' Arnold said, looking up.

'Mind your own fucking business,' Albert said. 'And stop yapping — I'm late.' He walked away.

Jack Trevor Story

'They were shacked up together,' Jeff told Arnold. 'Something nasty happened — you can guess what. Albert walked out on her.'

'Is that the one who came down here and smashed the place up? I heard about that.'

He could hardly have avoided hearing about it. Besides the broken window, the scars of Treasure's visit were everywhere in the shop — a cracked counter glass, a hole in the ceiling, an electric chandelier still festooned with broken globes.

Jeff laughed again. 'You should have heard her smashing the place up.' He talked across to Hetty, who was also smiling at the memory. 'How much damage did she do?'

'Hundred pounds' worth,' Hetty said. 'We're still stopping it out of Albert's wages — ' she broke off and frowned through her ledger. 'At least, we should be . . . '

She was remedying her neglect with pencil and rubber when Albert came back and found out what had happened. He swore at Jeff for mentioning Treasure just when everybody had forgotten her. 'I'm buggered if you'll have Mrs Wentworth now — not that she'd look at you.' He wheedled Hetty from her duty. 'Turn it in, sweetheart — I paid off forty quid and the old man's forgotten all about it.'

'Don't you believe it! She threw a toaster at him.'

'He doesn't know I'm not paying it off — another pound a week'll cripple me, honest!'

'Well . . . ' Hetty pondered over the books. 'If you get that washing machine back from Mrs Mason I'll call it quits — it's been on the dem list for three months and we've got the auditor in again next week.'

The three tally-boys became attentive and worried. It was the second time in a month.

'I know,' Hetty said. 'I don't know why he bothers — the auditor hasn't got a clue. Night and day for a week he worked — I ask you! A firm this size. I can do these books in me sleep. He doesn't seem to grasp this business any more than the last one did — and look where *he's* landed, in a loony bin!'

'I know what's in old Cally's mind,' Jeff said. 'He's got his eye on that place across the street — and you can't raise capital without audited accounts . . . '

Before they left on their daily rounds the talk got briefly away from sex and on to business. From their relative knowledge of the two subjects any sane auditor listening would have recommended a swift return to sex.

'I've got a switch job,' Arnold told Albert. 'Which cleaner do I take?'

'The one that's been noised-up of course — it's got red paint on the handle.' He switched on the old vacuum cleaner and shouted above the resultant din: 'For God's sake don't let them buy it — it cost fifty quid to get this racket without any suction. . . . '

The noised-up vacuum cleaner was the key appliance in the switch racket. Callendar's advertised reconditioned cleaners at seven-pounds-ten and followed up inquiries with a demonstration of this specially wrecked model. The housewives' understandable horror was then quickly alleviated by producing one of the new expensive machines on a no-deposit system. Switching the new for the old was a specialist piece of psychological selling and Arnold had not yet mastered the art.

'You'd better go along with him,' Albert told Jeff when the din had died away.

'We're getting bossy, aren't we?' Jeff muttered.

Arnold gestured him to silence. 'The key!' he whispered.

This was humorous patter which Albert was meant to overhear.

'Oh yes, of course,' Jeff said. 'Anything else you'd like me to do, old chappy? How about letting me reclaim that electric guitar? I know how sensitive you are about taking possession — sex apart, I mean.'

'Get stuffed,' Albert told him.

'That's what we were coming to,' Jeff said. 'The key, old chappy? It's Wednesday, y'know — early closing. Lots of little shop girls in the coffee bars with nothing else to do with their fannies except sit on them. Or had you forgotten?'

'You owe me ten bob each,' Albert told him. And when he had collected it: 'The key's under the mat. Go easy on the liquor and don't make too much noise — there's some new tenants underneath.'

'Are they any good?' Jeff asked.

'Niggers,' Albert said.

'Ugh!' Jeff said. 'How frightful! You'll have to move, old chappy. This town's getting loused out with them — it's no place for decent people. . . . '

Hetty at her desk was singing Beulah Land Sweet Beulah Land as Albert went out to load up his van. There was one good thing about Jeff and Arnold — they gave him a feeling of superiority which, in this business, you sometimes needed. Also mention of Treasure's name had given him a twinge of conscience and with it a sense of responsibility which might last for an hour or two. With this feeling still upon him he conscientiously checked his petrol and mileage readings before driving the heavily loaded Mini-Minor out of the yard.

As he turned into the dingy street Albert set himself a mental target of at least twenty calls, collecting and selling. He had done the same yesterday but had been sidetracked by a beautiful red-haired girl in a green swagger coat he had seen getting on a bus; he had followed the bus for miles, picked up the girl, taken her to lunch and afterwards spent five pounds on her in a shopping spree, finishing the day by taking her to a cinema, to dinner, and on an expensive pub crawl which had ended at Paul's drinking club. After all that he had failed to get her back to his room, struggled on the front seat for an hour without success and got home tired, frustrated, and ten pounds short in the kitty.

This was not going to be one of those days. He was going to be efficient and things were going to click. The people who were still dithering were going to buy; the people in arrears were going to pay up. He could be tough; when Jeff said he was afraid to re-possess goods from people who thought they could get away with paying when they felt like it he was being sarcastic. Albert was not afraid of anything except time, Monday and Tuesday had gone, but he still had the rest of the week. It was always a job getting started, but once he had he made up for it . . .

A fair-haired girl with a slim figure was walking in the shopping crowds along the main street. Albert looked round at her as he drove, then adjusted his mirror to see where she turned in. Well, there was no harm in starting the day with a coffee.

He parked in the first available space, checked his bow tie in the mirror, and combed his hair. When he entered the coffee bar the girl was sitting along at a table.

'Is this chair taken, miss?' he asked.

'No — nor are those,' she said, pointing to the vacant tables.

Albert laughed. 'That's what I like — a sense of humour. Haven't I seen you on the stage — are you at the theatre this week? You don't mind me sitting here, do you — I haven't got long. God, what a day — it's all go, isn't it?'

An hour later Albert ran back to his van, jumped in, stopped long enough to jot another name and telephone number into his book, then roared away. There were still four or five hours of the working day left. In fact, this was really the best time of the day to start if you wanted to find 'em at home. Albert could always justify whichever hour of the day he started as being the best hour, whichever day as the best day; whatever kind of a mess he got into he could, by torturing all the various alternatives, convince himself that it was a well thought out plan.

Besides, by this time Marjorie would've got the kids back to school. The twinge of conscience had gone and with it the sense of responsibility, the conscientiousness, the panic feeling in his stomach of being late; while the target for today had unified, simplified, and crystallized into one desirable bull's eye — Marjorie Mason and her fluctuating account.

4

IN the beginning there were two green hills outside the town; one steep and craggy with its back to the sun and its face to the smoke of the town and the winds of the north; the other gentle, undulating, prettily wooded and facing south. Of the two, from the point of view of human amenities and congeniality when it came to planning the vast council estate in the post-war slum clearance plan, the choice of hills should never have been in doubt.

It never was; the battlements of red brick houses were built upon the ugly hill with its view of smoke and chimneys, its coldness on a summer's day, its Siberian bleakness on a winter's day; its one-in-ten gradient which gave the old men coronaries and the young wives dropped wombs as they struggled against it with their heavy prams.

The gentle slopes of the other hill, green, bosky, and warm, were preserved; not by the town-and-country-planning-act or the green-belt or the fact of being a national monument or a national park, but simply because it was a Labour-council golf course.

Towards lunch-time Mr Callendar brought Reginald Corby into the clubhouse for a drink he had won. They seated themselves in wicker armchairs by the club windows overlooking the course, a large whisky apiece.

'I enjoyed that, Reggie,' Mr Callendar said.

'A nice round old man,' Mr Corby said, gratefully. He looked at his watch; he did not want to be stuck with Mr Callendar for lunch, quite apart from the cost. 'Haven't got time for more than one, though — business this afternoon.'

'And me,' said Mr Callendar. And after a moment: 'About that other business — I've got me feelers out.'

'Well you'll have to look sharpish,' Corby said 'There's

somebody trying for an option.'

Mr Callendar put down his drink and his hand trembled a little. 'You don't mean it!'

Corby smiled ruefully. 'Sorry, old man — nothing but the truth. Can't tell you who it is of course — ethics and all that.'

'Not a chain store, is it?' Mr Callendar asked, fearfully. 'I can't compete against those bloody crooks.'

'No — not a chain store. A local interest, I can tell you that — they're willing to go up to a hundred thousand pounds for the site if the deal goes through. Of course, it depends on planning permission and all that malarky.'

'And they want an option?' Mr Callendar said.

'Don't worry, it hasn't been granted yet — as a matter of fact I'm not advising it at present. An option can tie you up and stop competition.'

'Of course it can!' Mr Callendar exclaimed. 'You'd be stupid to grant an option on a site like that just when people are getting interested in it.' Trust my bloody luck, he thought, that people should be getting interested just as I make a start. The old factory had stood empty, uncared for and unwanted for ten years.

'Is it anyone I could join forces with?' he asked. 'I mean, if they're short of capital I might just be able to swing it — I wouldn't object to a partnership if they're the right sort of people.'

Corby shook his head and lowered his voice. 'It's not just a financial interest, old boy — it's commercial.'

'You mean they've got their own line?' Mr Callendar was depressed.

'I really can't tell you — sorry, old man. Like to, of course. Friends and all that. Could lose my place.'

'Is it radio and television?' Mr Callendar asked.

'No.'

'Is it furniture?'

'No — not furniture.'

'Have another whisky.'

'Thanks — no thanks. No. I'd better not — busy afternoon you know.'

'Too late,' Mr Callendar told him for he had ordered by signs. 'Tell me this then, Reggie — is it something they're likely to get planning permission on?'

Reggie Corby gave him a sorrowful, reproving glance. 'Now how would I know that, Cally old boy? I'm not on the council yet, you know' — he broke off to wave to a passing golfer just going out — 'he is, old Rogers. Got in on the swimming-pool ticket — luck that's all , happened to be a hot spring.'

'You'll get in, Reggie — it's a Labour community and they're short of good candidates. You know I'll help wherever I can — you can put your bills all over my vans and I'll help you with door-to-door canvassing.'

Reggie Corby sighed. 'It takes more than canvassing. Besides, Independent's the only thing — that's a clean word for Conservative in a town like this. The working class don't want the hard-hitting Labour candidate any more, old boy. Old boy.' He rubbed it in, self-mocking.

Corby was thirty-four, grey, full of self-interest, without any particular ability except the ability to impress an urbane personality on his clients. His ambitions lay beyond the limited horizons of a provincial estate-agents' office. His mother's ambitions for him were even greater — she saw him as at least a member of parliament. A great-uncle of hers had once been member for Hull and his brother Mayor of Cambridge before it was a city. In an effort to live up to their ancestors she had given Reggie a good education, sent him to riding lessons, and pushed him through his professional exams in the property business — which was as much as you could do unless you had direct county connections. He had repaid her by chaining himself to oblivion in marrying a common little working-class girl who happened to win a beauty contest which Reggie was helping to organize for the Labour club.

'Well, of course you're right, Reggie,' Mr Callendar told him. 'It's the working class that wield all the power today — what with their high wages and their unions and their strikes.'

'Second-hand aristocracy, old boy, that's what they

are. Biggest snobs in the country today, the working class. They don't want that "Living wage for the working man" stuff any more. Call anybody a working man today and he's insulted. He surrounds himself with the left-offs of his betters — second-hand Jaguars made for somebody else, big houses built for gentlemen, refrigerators, washing machines — well, you know better than I do. Half the riding schools are full of snotty-nosed gorblimey kids from the council houses — you don't know where you are these days. No quality any more, Cally.'

The remark about the second-hand cars had pricked Mr Callendar. 'Well, you'll never get in with a speech like that, Reggie.'

'You see who comes up here golfing at weekends — ruddy shopkeepers, factory foremen, cloth-cap oafs who don't know one end of a club from the other. Never have done before the war, you know. Nothing sacred now.'

'How about keeping the blacks out?' Mr Callendar said suddenly.

'What?' Reggie Corby was at sea for a moment.

'If you're looking for a ticket to get in on, I mean? There's a lot of anti-colour feeling. You've got to have a policy that'll appeal to a majority.'

'I dare say. Phew! That's the last thing. You try being anti-colour in print or on a platform — they'd stone you! You can think it but you mustn't say it — otherwise you're a black-shirt. No — nothing controversial, old boy. Good heavens, no! What?'

'There must be something,' Mr Callendar urged, anxious to be helpful in view of what Corby had told him about the pending option.

'All the best things have been used,' Corby said ruefully. 'Free school milk, open spaces, swimming pool — of course it has to be something that benefits their pockets, that's the only way to get a vote these days. But my God, you try to think of something they haven't got already — it's impossible.'

'How about touching their hearts?' Mr Callendar

suggested.

Reggie Corby laughed at the little man. 'We're being idealistic, aren't we?' He finished his drink and wiped his mouth. 'Well, have to go — '

'No, wait a minute — I mean it,' Mr Callendar said 'I was thinking of animals.' Corby waited, frowning. 'You see it really boils down to salesmanship,' Mr Callendar said, 'so it's not completely out of my line. You've got to sell yourself to the electorate with some kind of gimmick — right?'

'Yes, I suppose so.'

'Well, animal-loving in this country is like black-hating — if you see what I mean. People pretend they're not anti-colour — and people pretend they love animals. You've got to appeal to their pretence. Take dogs, for instance. We're all supposed to be dog lovers — I hate 'em, so do most people, but you can't afford to say so. I mean, they shit everywhere.'

Corby glanced around the club-house, nervously: 'What can I promise for dogs?'

Mr Callendar racked his brains. 'I don't know. There must be something. How about dog-drinking troughs on all the street corners?'

Corby thought about this for a moment and Mr Callendar watched him.

Reggie called for another drink and Mr Callendar smiled.

'I must say,' Reggie Corby said, slowly, 'it does show a bit of imagination, Cally old boy.'

Mr Callendar shrugged, modestly. 'It's not completely original, Reggie. Look at His Master's Voice — EMI, HMV. Where would they be without that little dog trademark? Look at Kosset Carpets and their cats — Baby Cham, British Lion, Kitty-Kat —'

'White Horse,' interjected Mr Corby, tipping his glass.

'Bunnyrugs!' said Mr Callendar, quoting a new line.

'Elephant and Castle!' Corby exclaimed.

They laughed together, finished their drinks and got up.

'I tell you what, Cally, old boy,' Corby said with a

new warmth. 'Why don't you drop in for cocktails about sixish? I'm having a few bods round — Major Simpkins, he's sponsoring me as candidate, you know old Simmy? I mean this might be what we're looking for. At least it does give us something to bite on — that reminds me, I must ring Joyce. About six, then?'

Reginald Corby was about to drive away in his big Bentley when Mr Callendar leaned in at the window.

'Is it a supermarket?'

'Eh?' Corby looked at him, blankly, for a moment, then smiled, chastisingly. 'Oh, the corner site — no, sorry old boy, can't say. It really isn't done, you know — ethics. Must preserve them. . . . '

Must preserve them! Mr Callendar thought, bitterly, watching Corby's car bumping down the hill towards the road. Cocktail parties! Bentleys! And his wife, to Mr Callendar's certain knowledge, heavily in debt. They hadn't even paid for their cocktail cabinet. Ethics! He knew the kind of ethics Reggie was waiting for — LSD. Otherwise why tell him about the option offer and then say that he had advised against it? He hadn't that much influence with Chas. Arthur Ltd, or his wife wouldn't be buying things out of a tally club. No, Reggie was waiting for Mr Callendar to do a spot of palm oiling. Well, it was a good job Mr Callendar had his ethics or he might — he just might — take out a summons against Joyce Corby before she had time to pay up her arrears. The threat of a county court action just before the council election would be more effective than a bribe.

But Mr Callendar turned away from the suggestion with a certain amount of pride and arrogance. And he wouldn't go in for a second-hand Bentley, either. He might be in the tally business now, but one day. . . .

5

JEFF JEFFERIES stopped his van outside one of the few detached houses in Archibald Road. He checked the number against the list in his book, then went round to the back of the van and pulled out a large carton bearing the blazoned name Wondersew. He was in the mood to sell something.

Luckily, tallying was the kind of job which catered for several moods; you could canvass, if you felt like it, knocking on strange doors and making new contacts, getting them interested in the whole range of goods; or you could spend the whole day collecting money if you felt belligerent; or you could, if you were in a technical mood, spend the day on dems — demonstrating this and that; or if it was an adventurous day you might pick one of the sure-selling gimmicks which demanded all your nerve and personality and come away with the customer signed up and another commission to be added to the week's harvest.

That morning's brush with the delightful Mrs Wentworth had whetted Jeff's appetite and sharpened his personality; he was ready for adventure.

On second thoughts the carton was too heavy to carry the length of a garden path and back again if there was nobody in; besides, it was psychologically good to break the news and then leave them waiting long enough to get them excited and anticipative. This was actually a third thought and untrue; it was just too heavy to waste time on. He walked up the garden path and rang the bell. He was relieved to find the housewife was young and attractive — it made his job easier. It made his smile easier; he glowed at her.

'Mrs Galletty? My name's Jefferies of Callendar's

Warehouse — I've got good news for you. . . . '

Mrs Galletty was not so young that she did not know a salesman when she saw one; without actually drawing back or closing the door or even losing her polite interest, she nevertheless stiffened, imperceptibly, summoning her sales resistance. She was twenty-four, well proportioned, two years married and her deceptively sleepy eyes were headlamps on an intelligent brain and a cynical sense of humour. She was a unilateralist from way back and had sat down tenaciously with the best of them in all kinds of uncomfortable places. Jeff couldn't possibly know it at this stage — that was the challenge of the job — but he had come to exactly the wrong person to try out the Wondersew lark. For one thing she knew all about it.

'Do you remember the Wondersew slogan contest we ran a few weeks ago, madam?' Jeff asked her. 'Well, I have to congratulate you — you're been very lucky!'

'Oh?' Her face slowly lightened and brightened with a thrill of sheer pleasure. Her husband, or any of the friends she had made in the old B-the-B campaign would have run at this stage. Jeff relaxed; the sale was as good as made.

'I've got the new Wondersew machine in the van now — you may care to be looking at the leaflet while I get it.' And producing the leaflet: 'You see it's an all-electric machine — straight sewing, embroidery, crochet, pleating, smocking —'

'You liked my slogan, then?' Mrs Galletty said. 'I hoped you would. You get the machine, I'll get the table ready — is it a three-pin plug or a two-pin?'

'I'll see to that, dear — just leave the door open. . . . '

When Jeff had gone back to his van, Mrs Galletty flew through her house and picked up the telephone.

'Daisy! He's here! Hurry up. . . . '

When Jeff came in with the machine the young woman was perched on the end of a settee with her legs crossed. 'You will have a cigarette, won't you? Coffee? I'll fix it while you're setting it up —' she gazed at the machine as he withdrew it from the carton, enraptured: 'It's really what I always wanted! Do you know I've never won anything before — fancy getting first prize!'

'Ah, well, your slogan was very good — brilliant, one of our directors said — but it didn't quite win first prize, darling. Very nearly, but not quite.'

Mrs Galletty looked puzzled. 'But I thought this was my prize?'

'Well, in a way it is, angel — you don't have to be disappointed. You are on ordinary mains, I suppose — two-thirty volts, fifty cycles. There, let's plug it in. . . .'

She waited. He plugged in the lead, turned a switch, got the machine humming. 'What do you think of that? Like a Rolls Bentley, isn't it? No interference with radio or television, either.'

'Well, is it mine or isn't it?' Mrs Galletty asked.

'Now a piece of material — any old panties? Give 'em to me and I'll embroider your initials on 'em — or mine!' He wrinkled his nose at her. 'No offence, I hope?'

'Tell me what I've won and I'll let you know!'

Jeff laughed at her, lit up cigarettes for both of them. 'That's the spirit!' He became confidential, generous, secretive. 'Now, look. sweetheart — I'll tell you the score. This machine as you know — look on the leaflet — costs fifty pounds. And very good value I might say! Why you could earn as much in six weeks with it —'

'I haven't got fifty pounds!' the young woman exclaimed.

'Of course you haven't — that's where your prize comes in. My firm is giving a ten pounds bonus to every runner-up in the slogan contest — this machine is yours for forty pounds! What do you say to that?'

'Just parcel it up and take it away, Mr Jefferies — '

'Ah-ah — wait for it! Not so fast!' Jeff got to the stage of putting his hand on her arm. 'Of course you haven't got forty pounds — who has, these days? You can spread it over two years at ten bob a week or nine months, if you want to clear it up quickly at, let me see — '

'No, thank you,' Mrs Galletty said, firmly. 'I wouldn't dream of getting into debt for a sewing machine — my husband would kill me!'

'Oh? He's like that, is he?' His grip tightened on her arm and he smirked. 'But perhaps you like 'em rough, eh?'

Mrs Galletty smiled. 'I can be rough, too.'

Jeff laughed, delighted. 'I like that! Nothing like a fight, I always say — did you know you've got wicked come-to-bed eyes?'

'Not green, I hope?'

'What?' Jeff detected wit and got back to business. 'Look, I'll tell you what I'll do — I like you. A nice sense of humour. Mind you I shouldn't do this — come over here.'

The young woman obediently followed him to the machine and he pointed to the sewing head. 'Look closely — you see those scratches? You can hardly see them, can you? But it is a little scratched — it's a demonstration model, you see. Quite as good as new — tried and tested of course. There's no fear of it ever giving you trouble now. But I can make a reduction for you.'

'How much?'

'Shall we say — five pounds?'

'Oh!' She turned away.

Jeff slipped an arm around her waist. 'Ten pounds?'

'It's too much still.'

He stood close behind her and ran both hands around her waist. 'I'll take off fifteen pounds — that means you get a fifty-pound Wondersew machine for half price. What d'you say?'

She was standing very still in his arms. 'Perhaps.'

The word seemed to have little to do with the transaction. Jeff tightened his hold on her. She strained away from him and he pulled her back. She turned swiftly and smacked his face with all the strength she could muster.

Jeff fell back, badly hurt, rubbing his face. 'Hey! What's the matter?'

'You assaulted me — I'm going to call the police.'

Jeff felt the ice in his stomach, suddenly knowing the score. The real score. 'Don't try that on me, dear — I've had some.' His voice trembled very slightly; the prospect of the *News of the World* could do this even to strong men who weren't married. 'Forget it,' he said. 'I'm going.' He started packing away the machine.

'Leave it where it is,' Mrs Galletty said.

Now he stared at her, his face still burning from the slap. This was new.

'Sign a receipt for twenty-five pounds and put my name on it.' She spoke calmly, watching him with her sleepy eyes.

Jeff laughed, harshly. 'What's this — a try-on?'

'No — just technique. You assaulted me — just touching me is assault. I shall make a complaint to the police unless you do as I say.'

'Don't be bloody silly — you've got no witnesses.'

'I only have to scream to get witnesses.'

Jeff turned white and the red finger-marks showed up vividly on his cheeks. 'Don't start screaming! That's a dirty trick!'

Mrs Galletty laughed. 'You think *that's* a dirty trick, do you, Mr Jefferies?'

'I'm going. . . . ' He had started packing the machine away again when she screamed, ripped her blouse open with one hand, tousled her hair with the other.

'You bitch!'

The door opened and a woman came in; she had been waiting for the scream. Jeff stared at her, dismayed. He knew her.

'Hello, Daisy,' Mrs Galletty welcomed her friend. 'This man assaulted me.'

'I know — I heard you scream. Dirty tyke — he tried it on me.'

'What are you doing here?' Jeff said.

But he already knew what she was doing there. He didn't know how it had been worked, but it had been worked. He had walked right into it.

'Now you listen to me, Mr Jefferies,' Mrs Galletty said. 'Daisy's husband went to prison because her little boy sent in one of your precious Wondersew slogans — oh yes he did! Summonses, judgement summonses, commitment — the lot. He went on short time and couldn't keep up the payments. Now you just sign the receipt.' She smiled at her friend. 'We'll flog it for what it's worth and share the proceeds — okay?'

'You could go to prison for this!' Jeff told them.

'But you've got no witnesses, darling, angel, sweetheart — lover boy!' Mrs Galletty told him.

Jeff opened his receipt book.

Crumbs! he thought.

The two women looked at each other across his bent bald head as he wrote. It would be something to giggle about at the next pacifist demonstration.

6

THE din and the debris, the roadworks and the demolitions taking place where the condemned roads of the town met the new developments all combined to give the noise, the appearance, and the activity of a grisly, barbarous battlefield where some bloody last stand was taking place.

A pioneer corps was busy with picks and shovels, a trench-digging machine lumbered back and forth like a blinded tank, heads in steel white helmets were moving to and fro in slit trenches while incongruously neat and natty gents were manipulating theodolites, aiming and sighting them like new slim-line machine guns at other young men who stood, unoffended, holding red-and-white striped poles and waiting, it seemed, to be shot.

On the fringe of this holocaust six terraced cottages stood in a row awaiting execution. Arnold Baxter stood at the door of one of these; he was holding the noised-up vacuum cleaner and banging a brightly-shone brass knocker. Behind him the god-awful row was punctuated by the staccato bursts of pneumatic-drills; banging the door seemed somehow superfluous — he couldn't even hear it himself.

It was some tortured moments before he noticed the neatly-printed card in the letter-box:

'Gone to the Garden of Rest — Miss Riley.'

Arnold thought about this for a moment; it conjured up various understandable possibilities; but then, remembering, he turned and scanned the square. On the far side of the raging battle an oasis of trees could be seen, shrouded at the moment in dust and smoke like a bizarre detail from the *Four Horsemen of the Apocalypse*.

Arnold replaced the cleaner in his van, then picked his way across the battlefield towards the garden.

The elderly and infirm inhabitants of the square sat in troupes in a rustic shelter in the garden, placidly chatting.

'Surely you remember Ada?' Miss Riley was saying to a woman companion. 'She was the wild one of the Frisbys. Always gadding off to funerals and such like. I don't believe she even had arthritis.'

'Was that the one who finally married that retired policeman with one kidney and a huge pension and went off to live at Worthing?'

'Now you've got her!' Miss Riley exclaimed. Then: 'What was I saying about her?'

'Look out!' her friend explained. 'Here comes old hot-rod!'

The two old ladies watched the approach of a motorized invalid carriage which came snorting across the square towards them, its driver leaning forward over the wheel, his beard, scarf, and hair flying in the breeze.

'Pretend you haven't seen him,' Miss Riley muttered. 'or we'll get bored to death with Villiers's engines and two-stroke three-wheelers . . .'

But hot-rod's target was the group of fellow motorized invalids at the far end of the shelter.

'They've condemned the tree!' he quavered, before

cutting his engine. 'They're going to chop it down!'

'Nonsense!'

'Poppycock, my dear fellow — they're just trying to demoralize you — '

'That's what it is — the Turks used the same tactics.'

'Then why have they painted a white cross on it?' hot-rod demanded. 'Don't take my word for it. Come and see for yourselves . . .'

The invalid carriages, pedalled, hand-driven, and motorized, all started into motion across the square, followed by a vanguard of bath-chairs pushed by faithful friends glad of the support.

'Did you hear that?' Miss Riley said. 'They're going to chop down the tree!'

'Come!' her friend pleaded. 'We must stop them!'

'Miss Riley!' Arnold called, meeting the group of elderly men and women as they hurried away from the shelter.

'I'm Miss Riley, young man?'

'I've got your vacuum cleaner — '

'It will have to wait, young man — ' her words came back to him as she trotted after the rest. 'They're going to chop down the tree . . .'

'Lot of bloody kids!' Arnold muttered, sauntering after them.

The approach of the elderly army, male and female, mechanized and foot, gradually, like a developing storm, stopped all work in the square. All eyes focused towards the big sycamore tree which a ranging theodolite had found to be standing in the direct path of a line of digging.

'Leave this to me,' said a sturdy foreman.

Others willingly fell back, including the workman who had painted the condemning cross on the tree and still held the whitewash brush, dripping guilty as blood into the bucket.

'Now, sir — what's all the fuss?' asked the foreman of hot-rod.

'You can't chop down that tree!' the old gentleman

said. And turning to the others: 'Can he?'

They all shook their heads.

'Why not, sir — if it's in the way?'

The old people looked at each other, speechless. If he didn't know, how could they tell him?

The sycamore tree had stood there longer than even the oldest of them could remember. It had been tall when the square was still green fields, the only traffic the passing of the seasons. Houses, shops, factories, streets, and paths had been built around it, deferentially and politely; sewers and mains had been laid a respectful distance from its roots. As children its bark had carried their sweetheart messages, as newly-weds its branches had tapped their bedroom windows; it was more than a tree, it was a totem, a family album, a familiar — and for some a monument and a memorial.

'You just can't, that's all,' hot-rod said, short of a reason.

'Where will all the birds go?' Miss Riley put in, helpfully.

'You'd better write to the council about it,' a surveyor suggested.

'We'll start a petition!' Miss Riley exclaimed.

'You do that,' said the foreman. 'Only you'll have to be quick. . . . '

Arnold cornered Miss Riley and led her back to the cottage, collecting the vacuum cleaner on the way.

'Of course, at seven-pounds-ten it's quite old, y'know, madam — not like a new one.'

'I prefer old things,' she said, letting him in. 'They'll never get away with it.'

'Just chuck a bit of dirt on the carpet,' Arnold said, as he plugged in. 'Then I'll give you a demonstration — only don't expect too much.'

'I haven't any carpets,' Miss Riley told him. 'You see it's not worth buying a carpet until they put me in the council flat — that's what they want to do. And I thought a bargain like this was too good to miss — you can try it on the lino.'

Arnold frowned; his training had been on carpet, not lino. Anything would pick up dirt from lino — even this old thing. He sprinkled sawdust on the floor of her parlour and she sat down to watch.

'You will clear it up afterwards, won't you?'

'Well, that's what this is supposed to do,' Arnold said.

'Switch it on, then,' she said. 'They'll just have to build round it — that's what they did before.'

The one way of getting her full attention, Arnold felt, was to switch it on. This he did — then screwed up his face at the noise. On the polished lino the old noised-up cleaner sounded like a squadron of aeroplanes. He looked round at her — and frowned again. Miss Riley sat watching and listening with a happy, but, at the same time, militant gleam in her eyes. She said something which he didn't catch and he was glad to switch off the machine.

'Blimey!' he said. 'This one's a bit noisy, isn't it?'

'I like it!' Miss Riley said.

'I beg your pardon?' He had a sudden awful thought: 'Can you hear all right? You're not deaf, are you?'

'Goodness me, no! The doctor said I have grade one acuity — I can hear every word they say next door if I press a tumbler to the wall and put my ear to it.'

'But you can't use a noisy machine like this, madam — it'd drive you nuts. I'll get on to them at the workshop when I take it back — '

'But you're not taking it back — I like it! I want it — and just look at the floor, all the sawdust has gone. I must try to get some sawdust.'

'There's a little still there,' Arnold said, lamely. 'Look, why don't you let me show you our newest machine and see the difference — I happen to have one in the van. Quiet as a kiss it is — '

'But it's the noise I like! Switch it on!'

Arnold switched the machine on again and the room was filled with the grinding of broken bearings and the clatter of asymmetric wheels.

'Listen!' Miss Riley cried.

From outside, as though competing with it, came the

roar of the tank and the clatter of the drills.

Miss Riley's eyes shone as brightly as her door-knocker; 'It's like fighting back!' she said.

Going out, having lost the firm's expensive dem model and with it his commission, Arnold met Miss Riley's friend coming in with a bundle of foolscap sheets.

'You must visit a lot of people,' she told Arnold. 'Will you collect as many signatures as you can and return it to me — you'll be helping to save the tree.'

'I'm sorry, but — '

Behind him Miss Riley had switched on the machine again. Arnold nodded, grabbed the papers and rushed away. The lady smiled gratefully after him, then popped her head into what could have been a high-pressure ball-bearing grinder.

'Are you there, Agatha?' she inquired.

Outside in the road a man operating a pneumatic drill was looking thoughtful; slowly he lowered his ear towards his machine to see if it was working. Even he knew Agatha was there.

7

ON the other hand Albert, more efficient, a better sales-man, and justifying Mr Callendar's belief in him as a brilliant tally-boy, had had more success than either Jeff or Arnold. Having by-passed the carpet he had already been on the bed with Marjorie Mason and was now getting off.

'Oh, good God,' she cried, 'look at the time — it's three o'clock!'

'School doesn't come out till half past four,' Albert said, 'and Sir won't leave till five.'

She spared him a glance from the mirror as she remade her face. 'I'm not talking about my husband, petal — I'm expecting the carpet man. Do you know fitted carpets cost the earth — I seem to have been paying for ten years! Do hurry, Albert — did you have to take your shoes off?'

'When I make love,' Albert said, 'I like to feel it means something. . . . '

She smiled at his reflection, tenderly: 'You are a petal, Albert. You're different from any of the others — do you believe that?'

'I rely on it,' Albert said, tying his laces.

Of his target of twenty calls he had made only one; he had made no sales and collected no money, but he felt better. Besides, Thursday was really the best day to start. People had more money on a Thursday, unless they had more money on a Friday.

'Can I take your washing machine in?' Albert asked when he was ready to leave.

She gave him a swift farewell kiss and straightened the bed. 'You marked it paid.' She thought for a moment. 'Or was that Sam?'

'It hasn't gone through the books yet — I just want to borrow it for stocktaking. Let you have it back in a few days.'

'Take it as you go out, then.'

'I don't think I can manage it by myself — not now.'

'But I don't want to get dressed!' She was wearing nothing.

'Slip your mac on,' Albert said, giving her a slap. 'Come on, hurry up!'

Together, hugging the washing machine, they went out of the house, down the garden path, across to the van, Marjorie trying to hold down the blowing mac with one hand.

'You could have put some shoes on,' Albert said, catching the movement of a curtain nearby. 'The neighbours are all at home.'

'There's not one of them got a home like mine, petal . . .'

Albert drove away, laughing.

At three o'clock that afternoon Reginald Corby was

telephoning his home.

'Joyce? I'm having a few friends in for cocktails this evening — now don't panic! There's plenty of drink. Rustle up a few canapes and we — that's right, canapes, snacks — won't you ever learn? All right, I'm not grumbling — but you've got to get used to this sort of thing — well, get mother over to put you right — all right. No, I can't get home early; I've got to go out — oh, and put on a decent dress — nothing common, no beads. Let's have a little class, shall we?'

He hung up and said, 'Christ!' then went to a hook festooned with keys and bearing the overall label: 'Furnished flats to let.' He selected a key with care.

A moment later he passed through the outer office of the Chas. Arthur establishment and threw a word to the receptionist.

'Back in about an hour, Shirley.'

'Yes, Mr Corby.'

'Shirl . . . ' the girl on the switchboard, sitting back to back with the receptionist, spoke without turning. 'Has he tried you, yet?'

'What d'you think — he's tried everybody.'

'One or two have never admitted it.'

'Don't be daft — they're the ones he succeeds with.'

Shirley looked to heaven. 'I shall never understand married men. I'd rather live with a bachelor.'

'She idolizes him,' the telephonist said. 'Hello, yes — Chas. Arthur estate office, putting you through. But he treats her like something the cat brought in. Of course, his mother doesn't help — Lady Muck.'

'I shall marry an orphan.'

'She's terrified of upsetting him. Just a moment, Mr Arthur, I'm ringing them for you. You should hear her when she rings him — you'd think she was asking for royalty instead of her own husband. "Don't disturb him if he's busy, I'll call later" . . . I'm putting you through now, Mr Arthur.'

'I wonder what she'd do if she knew what he was really like?'

'She'd never believe it. That kind never do — they build their whole existence round their heroes. She daren't even ask him for money. She thinks he's a saint and she's got to live up to him.'

'I'd like to tell her the truth.'

'That wouldn't be any good — she'd have to have her nose rubbed in it. Chas. Arthur estate office . . . '

It was almost as much as anybody could ever hope to know about the private life of the Corbys.

Joyce Corby was counting the remains of her house-keeping money when Albert arrived at the door. Had she known who it was she would not have answered the bell, but it was mid afternoon and she was not expecting any more callers after money. She opened the door, still holding her solitary pound note and wondering how she was going to make it provide snacks — canapes, rather — and also stretch to the end of the week.

'You owe more than a pound, Mrs Corby,' Albert told her. 'It's four weeks now.'

She screwed the pound note up, protectively: 'Oh, this isn't for you, Mr Argyle — I mean, it's all the change I've got and I've got to do some shopping with it.' Got, got, got, Reggie would say. The word got is only permissible in certain contexts, otherwise it's vulgar. 'I'm terribly sorry — would you mind waiting one more week till I get some change?' Never say you haven't any money — especially to tradespeople; say you haven't any change at the moment.

'Can't let it go another week, dear — madam. Sorry. I'd get the sack!' Albert felt sorry for Mrs Corby and always wanted to call her dear; not that he wanted to make her, she wasn't the kind. Sex wasn't by any means the usual thing on the tally-boy round; they were always looking for it, ready for it, but there weren't more than half a dozen Marjorie Masons in his whole territory. Most married women weren't interested in it any more; either it bored them or they loved their husbands or they looked down on tally-boys. The sort that were going to play you could tell from the first glance, the first half-dozen words; as for the rest all the charm in the world wouldn't soften them, it would only bore them.

Of course there were all sorts of other relationships; there was the chummy relationships or the gossipy one or the cup of tea and cake one. But this one had always been Mrs Corby and Mr Argyle, even though they were much of an age and came from the same background. Albert had always felt a bit sorry for her; she was pretty, but she seemed lonely and out of her depth in this luxury flat, like a cat in a lion cage. She tried to put on airs, but she was tense and worried and couldn't quite pull it off. Also, not having the weekly instalment embarrassed her; had she been in the same class as the flat she would carry her debts with a fine careless flourish of unconcern. Albert knew that type and could deal with them with a few careless flourishes of his own. But Mrs Corby, while calling him Mr Argyle and keeping her distance, at the same time appealed to him in a mute way. Her grammar, her speech, her uncertainty and lack of self-confidence brought her as close as the girl in the tobacco kiosk; the flat and her feeble pretences, which she seemed unable to believe in herself, held them apart.

'Who's that for then?' Albert said, indicating the pound note. He would never have asked such a question of the class of woman she was trying to be.

'I got to get some stuff in for a party,' she said. She would never have told him if she had really been the educated woman Reggie should have married. 'Canapes,' she added, carelessly. 'And that.'

'Well, what's most important?' Albert said.

'I'm ever so sorry,' she said, wretchedly. 'Only he's — my husband's holding a cocktail party for some friends. It's business.' She bit her lip, returning to the other problem for a moment. 'Dunno what I'm going to give them.'

'You want to get somebody in to help — a cook or something.' Albert often found himself worrying for her, in spite of her attempt to be stand-offish.

'Are you kidding!' she said.

Then she broke off and smiled artificially over his shoulder. A lady from the flat above was going across the carpeted landing. 'Good afternoon, Mrs Jenkins — lovely now!' she called, in an artificial voice to match the smile. And then to Albert: ''ere — you better come in. He don't like — my husband objects to washing the dirty — discussing private affairs where the neighbours can hear. Their ears are always flapping.'

'There's no point my coming in if you haven't got the money.' The sentence rang strangely in Albert's own ears; he couldn't think of many pretty blonde girls he would have said it to.

'Supposing I can get some change tomorrow — would that be all right — ' Joyce Corby stopped speaking again as the neighbour walked back. Albert, by silent mutual agreement, went into the flat with her.

She looked at the clock. 'I dunno though — half past three. It's a bit late.'

'The banks are shut,' Albert said. 'But I'll take a cheque if you like.'

'What?' she said. 'Oh, well, I don't think I've got a cheque. He keeps — my husband has the cheque book.'

'Get him to write a cheque out tonight and I'll call —'

'He wouldn't do that! I mean, I couldn't ask him. Not very well. You see, I manage all the weekly accounts and so on.'

'Does he know about them?' Albert asked, baldly.

'Oh, well, not the details. He gives me ten pounds a week and I have to manage — of course, it's ample, really. Only I'm not very good at it. Money seems to run away — d'you know I went into the supermarket this morning and got through twenty-five shillings without seeing a thing for it! Just a packet of soap flakes, tin of salmon, tea, coffee, shampoo, and chocolates — nothing you could really make a meal out of!'

She had forgotten the distant relationship and was immersed in the awful morass of her own misery. She was glad of somebody to talk to and Albert sat on the arm of a chair to listen, sympathetically; it was a story he knew well.

'You want to get a system,' he said, earnestly. He felt methodical again. 'What are your weekly payments — tally clubs and so on?'

'About four pounds altogether — including the bedroom suite in his — in my husband's room. He's got this quilted plastic headboard — it's really lovely.'

'You don't have to pay for all that, do you?'

'I do now. But of course he started most of the things off with a deposit — he's very good really. Only now he's got the Bentley — he had to have it when they made him junior partner — '

'Blow that,' Albert exclaimed, indignantly. 'Why don't you ask for a rise! You're stupid, you are, madam,' he added, remembering himself momentarily.

He was infected by the odd way she had of talking about her husband as though he were a V.I.P. employer; they might easily have been two dissatisfied members of the staff.

'Now they're talking about taking his bed back. I don't know where he's going to sleep! I believe he thinks it's paid for.'

'How long have you had it?' Albert asked her.

'About nine months — '

'How much have you paid off it — if it's more than half they can't touch it without a court order. Let me have a look at your card, dear.'

As she went to a writing-bureau Albert went on: 'You should've got it from us, you know.' It didn't occur to him that he was encouraging a bad account in his own books. She came and sat in the chair with him and together they added up the payments.

'There you are, you see — they can't touch it! You write them a stinking letter — in fact if you wait till to-morrow I'll dictate it for you. Then every time they threaten court proceedings, send 'em the odd five bob — you can stall 'em off for years if you know what you're doing.'

'It's very good of you!' she said. 'What with that and the distraint warrant I didn't know — '

'Which distraint warrant?'

'Well, it hasn't come yet — it's about a suit he had — my husband got. A long time ago. They're coming to distrain on the furniture for it — I don't know what he'll say if he finds out!'

'Whose name was the suit in?' Albert asked.

'Mine. It was a present, you see.'

'Whose name is the furniture in?' Albert asked, business-like. 'I mean have you got anything in your husband's name — anything at all?'

'Only this three-piece his mother give him,' she said. 'Why?'

'Do you know if she's got the receipt?'

'Yes — it's in the bureau.'

'You're all right then, dear — when the bums come to mark the stuff up, tell them to distrain on the three-piece and give them the receipt to cover it. They can't touch it! You won't hear another word about distraint after that — they won't even pursue it to court, it'd cost 'em money.'

Joyce Corby laughed up at him in sheer relief. 'It's not so bad when you know all the ropes, is it?'

'They can still hang you!' Albert said. He stood up. 'Okay tomorrow, then?'

Worry fitted across her face again. 'I'll try — I'll see what I can do if I hurry. I've got this part-time job — '

'Part-time job!' Albert exclaimed. 'If you ask me you've got a full-time job here — and I thought you had a cocktail party tonight?'

'Well, I can't promise about the money,' she said. 'Will you be angry if you come tomorrow and I haven't got it?'

Albert laughed at her, touched. 'I don't know how anybody could be angry with you — you're just a kid and you're right in it, aren't you? You don't want a husband, you want a father. You shouldn't let chaps like me fright-en you, y'know.'

'I'm always frightened,' she admitted. 'I hide in the

Jack Trevor Story

bathroom sometimes when the bell goes.'

'I know you do, dear,' Albert said. 'And you're not the only one.'

'Would you do me a favour, Mr Argyle?' she asked, suddenly. And at his nod: 'Would you tell me which dress to wear tonight?' And before he could respond: 'Just wait here a minute.'

He watched her go into a bedroom. 'Blimey,' he muttered. 'What's the matter with me?'

Joyce came out of the bedroom with two dresses, holding them up. 'I like this one, but I'm not sure.'

'Slip it on,' Albert said.

'Look the other way, then.' She unzipped her skirt and stepped out of it.

Albert turned away, obediently, lighting a cigarette and one for her. The next moment she was twirling in a flowered, flared dress in front of him.

'Not that one,' he said. 'Too much frilly petticoat — it's pretty, mind you — I'd go a bomb for you. But it's not a cocktail party with him and his pals. More the palais or the pictures or a quick snog in the woods. Haven't you got something straight — black, say?'

'Just a minute.'

Albert dressed her in a simple straight-cut black dress with a straight top shoulderless bodice and strings.

'Marvellous!' he said. 'When you've got curves always wear straight dresses. Of course you want dark stockings, high heels and your hair up — '

'I was going to have it down — '

'No no — come here. . . . '

He sat her down, got busy with a comb.

'Where did you learn to back-comb?' she asked.

'I used to do this for Treasure,' he said.

'Is that your girl?'

'She was till she found out about me — she hates me now.'

'I bet she doesn't really.'

Albert dwelt on the thought as he worked at her hair.

'Treasure's a nice name,' she said.

'It's only what I call her. Her name's Teresa Hunter — Treasure Hunter, get it? She's the give-away girl at the Bingo Hall. Well built too — plenty of superstructure. Treasure chest!'

Joyce Corby laughed. Then sympathetically she said: 'Was it another chap?'

'No — abortion. You know, usual sordid mess. And she's very sensitive.'

'Poor thing.'

'Oh, I dunno,' Albert said. 'That's the trouble with women — you always get involved and then you're stuck.'

Joyce Corby sighed, turning her head this way and that as he shaped her hair. That's what had happened to poor Reggie; she should never have married him. She was only a drag on him. She had mucked up his whole life. He couldn't stand her friends and his friends seemed to stay away from her. And if his mother came she always made her feel like sixpence.

'There you are, Mrs Corby — you look lovely and don't let anybody tell you you don't!' Albert stood admiring his handiwork.

Joyce looked at herself in the mirror, just to turn the tears of self-pity away from him.

Albert came behind her. 'What are you crying for?'

The tears came faster at his gentle tone. 'I always blub if people are kind to me. . . . '

Albert gave her his breast-pocket hankerchief and she blew her nose, noisily.

Albert was touched; uncomfortably touched. The only time Treasure had cried was when she lost the baby — and after months of trying to lose it. It wasn't even a baby. It hadn't affected him much at the time; but each time he had thought about it since it had affected him a little more. Now, seeing Joyce Corby cry it was as though it had all happened again only this time it was digging into him.

'Don't cry. You'll be all right, love.'

'Sorry, Mr Argyle.'

'Call me Albert — Maison Albeeerr, coiffures for mesdames!'

'I'd better not,' she said, but smiling now and tucking the handkerchief back into his pocket. 'I might let it slip out — he doesn't like me — my husband doesn't like me making new friends. Outside his — ring — circle. You know.'

'You don't sound very happy with him — '

'Oh, no,' she broke in, quickly, 'he's a wonderful husband — it's just me, that's all. I mean, I'm not educated or anything — he went to a good school — mind you he never talks about it, he's not a snob or anything. But he likes things proper — properly done, I mean. He's trying to get on, you see. He's putting up for the council. He brings all sorts of people here. That's why I have to keep the place nice. Of course, it costs a lot. Glasses, silver, serviettes — I mean napkins. Men don't realize, do they? It all has to be paid for — and Reggie — that's his name — my husband — don't — I mean doesn't believe in debts. He's got very high principles — ethics. No, principles. Is that right?'

'Don't ask me! Jesus — if he gets you mixed up like that what's he going to do with the council?'

'It's me, not him! It's I, I mean. Oh dear. I always wanted to better myself — he's only trying to help me. I don't mind. I mean, I want to be a credit to him. If a man's going to get on in local government and all that a wife's very important to him. That's what his mother always says.'

Albert's heart went out to her. 'And what does your mother always say?'

'They're dead — I've only got a sister. She lives up on the council estate. He doesn't — my husband doesn't like me visiting her. She's married to a bus driver.'

'He sounds delightful!'

'Who — oh, George?' Her face brightened with enthusiasm. 'Oh, he is — he's a scream. Ever so kind to the kids — or do you mean — '

'Skip it,' Albert said. He reset a piece of hair which had fallen on to her forehead and said: 'Can I ask you a personal question? Why do you have separate bedrooms?'

She didn't mind answering; she could have been gossiping with an old schoolgirl chum. 'His mother doesn't think we should have any children until he's properly established. You see, we had one or two near squeaks in the beginning.'

Albert smiled at her, appraisingly, mock-wicked: 'I can believe it!'

'Don't be cheeky!' She was enjoying the compliment.

'He's not playing the field, is he?' Albert asked.

'What, Reggie?' There was a small element of scorn in her voice and she was shocked by it. 'Certainly not! You don't know him. He's very strong-minded about that sort of thing.'

'I don't know how you live up to him,' Albert said.

'It's because he's worth it,' she said, simply. 'I'd do anything for him.'

Albert sighed, ruefully: 'Some fellows get all the luck.' He looked at the time and groaned. 'See you tomorrow, then?'

'Are you going, then?'

''Fraid so. Running late. It's all go, isn't it?'

'Thanks for doing me hair and that,' she said. 'It was nice to have somebody to talk to — I don't feel half so worried as what I did. Will you write that letter to them people for me tomorrow about the bed?'

'Sure,' Albert told her. She looked lonely now that he was going and he smiled at her, reassuringly. 'Cor! You look terrific — is it right you were a beauty queen?'

She blushed with pleasure. 'Who told you that, then?'

'My spies, of course — why do you think I come canvassing in the first place?'

Joyce laughed at him. 'You're a tonic, Mr Argyle! Fancy you knowing that. I was Miss Agricultural Tractors two years running — that's how I met him — my husband. He was the host at the Labour club where they give us dinner — I drank half a bottle of champagne!'

'He knew what he was doing!' Albert said. 'Still,' he added as a serious bit of advice from kind to kind, you want some real friends, too, y'know. I mean, these toffy noses are all right, I suppose, but they're all the same — estate agents, solicitors, bank clerks, all on the grind, all in each other's pockets in a town like this. I mean, you go in the lounge of the Marquis and listen to 'em — "haw haw with their little caps and old school blazers, what".'

Joyce laughed aloud; it was not a modulated or cultured sound. It was a laugh. She was not sufficiently self-analytical to know that she was laughing the tension out of three years with Reginald; it did not occur to her that they were both talking about Reginald.

'You're too good for them, you are. We're flesh and blood, we are. They wouldn't know what to do with a real woman. You don't go for tea and a chinwag in Mary's Pantry, do you? 'Course you don't! My Christ, what a lot of horse-faced hockey-stick horrors they are!'

Joyce laughed again; she was laughing at Reginald's mother without realizing it.

'Of course, they're all as phoney as arse-oles,' Albert said, 'if you'll forgive *le mot juste*. I mean, they're as lady-like as hell on sherry, but you get a few vintage ciders into them when the old man's not around and see 'em get their finger-nails in your back!'

'Oooo! Mr Argyle! They don't! Do they?'

Albert put his finger to his lips: 'No tales out of school! But I tell you this — you want to watch yourself at that cocktail party tonight. You're the kind of dish they think about when they're in bed with their missis!'

'I don't have to worry,' Joyce said. 'He'll be there — my husband. Else I wouldn't trust meself alone with that horrible Major Simpkins — he keeps patting my hand!'

'That's what I mean,' Albert said. 'Bloody insult! If he was half a man at all he'd pat your bottom, wouldn't he? They haven't got the courage of their convictions.'

Joyce was still laughing immoderately when she saw Albert out of the flat. It always gave Albert a feeling of success to leave them laughing; whether he had sold anything or not, whether he'd collected long-standing arrears or not, whatever the dismal state of his personal finances or whatever catastrophe threatened, some deep theatrical instinct, deeper than care, was satisfied if he could leave them laughing. It was perhaps the applause that he badly needed, a measure of his charm and likeability. It was what hurt him most about the affair with Treasure; that in the end, after all the laughs they had had, he had left her hating him.

'Well, you know what they say,' he told her as a parting shot on the landing, unaware that Mrs Jenkins was again — with furtive purpose — going or coming. 'We put up with the same thing day after day for the sake of the same thing night after night!'

'Ooooo!' Joyce cried, with a laughing pretence at being outraged.

'Ta ta, love!' Albert called as he ran down the stairs.

'Toodle-oo!' Joyce Corby cried, adding, as she saw her neighbour's shocked face, 'Mr Argyle!'

'Good afternoon, Mrs Corby!' Mrs Jenkins made it sound like an accusation and a reminder as she passed by the door.

Horse-face, Joyce thought. She went back into the flat and crossed to the window. She was not in the mood to be intimidated now. Why should she better herself? Albert had made her feel that she was already the right kind of person and, what's more, in the majority. She looked down as Albert was opening the door of his van; he looked up and waved and she waved back. A young police constable was proceeding along the opposite side of the road and she heard their shouted greetings.

'Up your pipe, Albert!' called the policeman.

'And you, Sid!' Albert replied, sticking up two fingers.

It warmed Joyce to hear the friendly exchange. Mr Argyle was right; from the eleven-plus onwards there were two kinds of people in the world — her sort and his sort. Her husband's. Reginald's. And she was beginning to feel — first prize or no first prize — that inter-marriage was wrong.

When Joyce had watched Callendar's little van speed away, she closed the window and sat down to review her problems. Now that he had gone she felt completely cut off again. It was a lovely flat, tastefully decorated and furnished with fitted carpet, Regency chairs and settee, scraps of wrought iron holding flower vases and lamps, delicate bits of china and pottery, the latest coalglow electric fire and a pair of good reproduction paintings of horses each side of the mantelpiece; in fact the room had come straight out of a *Homes and Gardens* photograph and it was just the kind of place she had dreamed of having while she was working in the Agricultural Tractors factory office. But the part of it not in the dream was that she would be alone in it most of the time and worrying about paying for it. What was the good of a house of cake if there was nobody to share it with and if you had to pay for it?

'I'll have to give him something,' she told herself, looking at the paltry pound note which wouldn't go anywhere. She was thinking of Mr Argyle and his kindness and patience. 'And I'll have to give them something,' she added, remembering the cocktail party.

She looked at the clock, then went to the telephone, driven to an inescapable solution which she would never have dreamt of if it hadn't been available and convenient in the town.

'Is that the Confidential Secretarial Service? Miss Alcott? This is Joyce — have you got a part-time job I could do before five o'clock?' she asked.

'As a matter of fact I think I have,' came Miss Alcott's voice. 'Pamela's let me down — but you'll have to get cracking right away!'

'I'm coming now,' Joyce told her.

She slipped on her nylon-fur coat and as an after-thought cleaned her teeth. 'When it comes to helping her husband,' Joyce liked to remember Reginald's mother saying at this particular stage of what had become her life, 'it's a wife's job to do everything she's capable of, no matter how little that may be.'

And she rushed out to do it.

8

MISS ALCOTT'S flourishing call-girl service was the result of a happy chance. Elizabeth Alcott was the daughter who stayed at home to look after her parents until either they died or she did. This left her forty-eight, straight as a board, Victorian in her conversation and outlook, completely inexperienced with men but with a rudimentary knowledge of cats. During the last ten years as nurse and companion to her surviving parent, her father, she had learned touch-typing to provide for the future. She had gone twice a week to night classes at the technical school, sitting with a class of young girls, her hands hidden by a cover while she memorized the home keys.

Alone at last to earn a living in a town whose materialistic values were far removed from Queen Victoria's, she had spent her small legacy on a good reconditioned typewriter, a second-hand electric duplicating machine and the lease of one of the little dingy derelict offices which had once been part of a ribbon factor's establishment. It was an appropriate place; the Victorian office and the Victorian lady were in business.

Miss Alcott ventured a small advertisement in the local press and distributed cards around the newsagents' boards then sat back and waited. The first week brought her one boy scout who offered ten shillings to have a jumble-sale circular typed and duplicated. After this she typed a few letters for people who wanted to impress or were writing for jobs or in debt and hoping to convince their creditors that they were not poor and helpless. The first month brought her a gross of three pounds five and a net loss of ten pounds sixteen — she had ample time to do her books meticulously.

Oddly enough it was at this time that she had got into trouble with the police for the most, she considered, obscure reason. They had arrived at her office in two squad cars — a detective superintendent, an inspector, and four or five other ranks. They had with them a copy of what up until then had been her most lucrative job — a twenty-page booklet which she had been paid ten pounds for by some nice young man. She had set it out neatly, typed it most accurately and artistically with both margins straight-edged right down the pages. She had run off fifty copies from the stencils and bound them in blue covers with pretty gold-tinselled string to hold them together. The young man had been very pleased and had promised to recommend her to all his friends, especially as she had been diplomatic enough to tell him how much she had enjoyed reading it when in fact, apart from some pleasant jingles which were reminiscent of nursery rhymes, she had not understood a word of it.

'Did you print this, madam?' the superintendent had asked her. Then, at a second glance: 'Or did you allow somebody to use your machine?'

'I did it myself,' Miss Alcott said, proudly. 'Is anything wrong?'

It was pornography of the crudest kind. The sex act put to rhyme in a dozen different ways; new positions set to old rhythms, organs put to music, anecdotes in bio-logical detail, exploits legendary and apocryphal in which pelvic cavity rhymed with depravity in a saga of filth and four-letter words unknown in Miss Alcott's vocabulary.

'It's a little anthology,' she told the C.I.D. man. 'Most of it rather over my head, though I do appreciate its merit. I'm not much of a one for modern verse, though of course I know what I like.' And then, seeing the glances the policemen were exchanging, she said, nervously: 'It's not political, is it?'

'No madam,' the superintendent told her. 'But if that young chap ever comes in again, ring the police station and then lock yourself in the back room.'

Miss Alcott was never certain what exactly was wrong with the booklet, but to be on the safe side she had taken the sample copy out of her specimens book; when she came to think of it it might explain why the Vicar of Little St Paul's had changed his mind about giving her the parish magazine to duplicate.

After this she had become over-cautious about accepting manuscripts from authors and refused to type them unless she fully understood the context; as it sometimes took weeks of reading and research for her to understand the simplest stories and as authors objected to being cross-examined about their work, the business gradually fell off, from being almost nothing, to nothing.

It was then that Miss Alcott discovered a small but steady demand for the services of a typist who could attend at under-staffed offices. She took to doing morning work here and there, filling in during summer vacations and generally obliging local business people. Sometimes she found that she was wanted in two places at once and by advertising she was able to contact other women who could help out and who were willing to pay her ten per cent of what they earned for the convenience of having their part-time work organized for them.

As this business began to build up, so more typing came in, for she had made some personal contacts and was ready to accept office overflow work. To increase this work so that she could spend as much time as possible in her own office — the dingy place suited her and she liked it — she expanded the agency to include domestic workers, locals and continentals *au pair*; she took on the tedious business of addressing thousands of envelopes for direct mail advertising for people like Callendar's Warehouse with an extra fee folding leaflets, putting them in, stamping, and posting. From all this, if she worked a twelve-hour day, never looking up, she found that she could average, from commissions and direct earnings, above ten pounds a week gross, five pounds net. Just enough to live on and keep the cats.

Then, quite fortuitously, she had been put on to what seemed like — to Miss Alcott — a good thing. She was always looking for a good thing; the part-time office work was a good thing, so was the direct-mail envelope addressing. Anything for which she could see a steady demand until she was old enough for a pension looked like a good thing. This good thing had come about when one afternoon one of her married women part-time typists had come into the office crying and deeply distressed. That morning Miss Alcott had sent her to work for a local historian, a nice old gentleman who was compiling a history of the town and borough with particular reference, Miss Alcott gathered during her usual screening, to the town's past association with the textile industry.

'He attacked me,' the woman said, between her sobs.

'Mr Weatherhead? I can't believe it! Do you mean he tried to kill you?'

'He tried to get my clothes off!'

'Whatever for?' Miss Alcott exclaimed.

'What do you think?' the woman said angrily.

Miss Alcott had no idea; the woman, with a family and a considerable hire-purchase commitment, was badly in need of the work and impatient with Miss Alcott's simlicity.

'Don't you know anything about — life? He wanted me. He wanted to — to cuddle me.'

'Perhaps he's grown fond of you?' Miss Alcott suggested. The romantic stories in *Christian Girl* were her only vaguely remembered authority on such matters.

'I've never been there before!'

'But you've been there all day, dear,' Miss Alcott said. 'Besides, he's quite well-known locally.'

'Then I think you might have warned me!' the woman said, bitterly. 'If I told my husband he'd get six months!'

'Don't bring the police into it!' Miss Alcott cried, with the fear of one who, although completely innocent and unaware, already has a record.

The next day she had happy occasion to telephone the woman. 'Have you told your husband about Mr Weatherhead?'

'No — he wouldn't believe nothing happened if I told him.'

'Well as long as nothing happened I shouldn't tell him, dear — Mr Weatherhead has just called in and left five pounds for you! He wants you to go again!'

'When?' the woman asked.

That's how it had started. The word had spread, at first between Mr Weatherhead's close circle of friends and later to a wider clientèle. Because of her innocence Miss Alcott was able to build up the business into a good thing much faster than somebody who knew exactly what she was doing.

'Is it private and confidential work at your home?' she would ask, coyly. 'Then you want somebody attractive — I know!'

She knew nothing. Until Mrs Christie told her a few things. Mrs Christie was one of Miss Alcott's busiest part-time workers and she had been sitting in the office one day when a telephone conversation was taking place.

'I can't make it less than two pounds for half an hour — plus her bus fare of course. . . . '

'You take a few risks, don't you — talking like that over the telephone?' Mrs Christie had said, afterwards. 'If anybody gave you away you'd get five years!'

'I don't understand!' Miss Alcott said.

Mrs Christie, once she believed Miss Alcott didn't understand, explained at length. It took a great deal of explanation, for she had to cover in half an hour or so what should have been covered over the past forty years.

'You mean — like cats?' Miss Alcott whispered, as the light began to gleam.

It said much for Miss Alcott's determination, strength of character, and Victorian stoicism, that once she learned the gravity of the crime she was committing in running business premises for an illegal purpose she did not panic or faint, but took all her records and burnt them.

A few months later she moved into a suite of new offices over a bank in the main street and resumed the typing and duplicating business as a necessary front. Financially it was unnecessary, for the call-girl business was bringing in a clear eighty pounds a week profit; there were so many men like Mr Weatherhead and so many young wives who needed the money.

Besides — and this was Miss Alcott's secret — because of the way she had started she had the knack of making prostitution seem a respectable and necessary amenity in the Welfare State. No matter what had been explained to her, it would always be part-time work. The men seemed to like it, the women seemed to need it, so there couldn't be anything very wrong in it.

'Here's the key, dear,' she told Joyce Corby when she came in this afternoon. 'It's fourteen Grosvenor Court — he's been on before and he sounds rather distinguished, but don't forget to pick up the fee before you let him stroke you. . . . '

Miss Alcott still had only the vaguest idea what actually went on and she wasn't terribly interested now.

Joyce Corby's first qualm of fear came when she saw the well-known board outside the block of flats at Grosvenor Court: 'Furnished Flat to let: Apply Chas. Arthur, Auctioneers and Estate Agents.'

She hesitated in the forecourt. If it was to let, why was somebody apparently living there? And if somebody had moved in recently, did they know him — Reginald, her husband? It was unlikely. And even if they did it was more unlikely that they would know her. She was the last person he would introduce prospective clients to. She had never met one of Reginald's clients. On this thought Joyce went to the lift and pressed the button. Why shouldn't she meet one of his clients? It would just serve him right meeting them like this and he not knowing! They were always lords or ladies, sheriffs or millionaires, according to him — Reginald. He was a great name dropper — it went with the business. She wasn't criticising him for it. It was just aggravating that he never brought the famous ones home for cocktails so that she could have a bit of excitement in a dull life.

As she went up in the lift, she saw a possible small scene taking place at the breakfast table.

'Yes, I showed Sir Arthur over the Grosvenor Court flat — he was quite taken with it. Nice chap, asked me to play a round of golf sometime.'

'Well, why don't you, dear? I slept with him yesterday and we got on very well together.'

No need to say it was only for half an hour and that he'd paid her three guineas. She could just imagine his face!

On the third floor Joyce walked along to number fourteen and hesitated outside the cream-painted door. It was a very expensive flat. She tapped, then listened at the door for a moment. She could hear the sound of running water. It was the bath routine. Well, it was always nice to know they were clean living. There was one thing — apart from a baby — which she would never be able to explain away.

Using the key, she let herself into the flat.

The scene was set as for a play. Dim lights, the curtains drawn to keep out daylight, a fire glowing. A table against a big divan, lush with cushions. Drinks on the table. Through a green glass partition the sound of running water and the silhouette of a man taking a shower. Joyce went to the settee, kicked off her shoes, flung off her coat, settled down on the settee. She studied the bottles for a moment — whisky, gin, vermouth sweet and dry. The three pound notes were tucked under the gin bottle, the three shillings alongside. Joyce picked up the money and put it into her handbag, gratefully. It would provide Mr Argyle with his arrears and the cocktail party with its snacks. Canapés.

Joyce helped herself to a gin and French, drank it quickly, then filled up again before calling:

'I'm here!'

The water stopped running.

'Hello?' said a man's voice. 'Is that you, darling? With

Jack Trevor Story

you in a minute!'

Joyce jumped to her feet, spilling the drink. She picked up her coat and then looked for her shoes. One she found and put on.

'Make yourself comfortable, darling!' came the voice again. The familiar voice, though not in any familiar tone; a voice that had criticized her, picked her up on a million points of etiquette and grammar; a voice cultured, mannered, sophisticated. The voice of him. He. Reginald. Her husband.

'Honest to God!' Joyce exclaimed, petrified.

'Are you all right?' came the voice again.

'I can't find my bloody shoe!' Joyce muttered. She started groping round on her knees in the gloom.

'Come and join me if you like!' He had half-opened the door.

This was Reginald who had told her off for opening the bathroom door when he was there. It was un-ethical. Or un-something. Now she found the shoe and hurried towards the outer door.

'Is that Pamela?' came the voice. 'Or Joan? Strip off, darling — we haven't much time, have we?'

Joyce closed the door behind her and ran.

'Coming soon! . . . ' Her husband's voice followed her, fruity with passion.

9

BY half past five Albert was driving back towards the warehouse, the day's work nearly done. He had not met the brave target he had set himself, he had sold nothing beyond a bit of counter business with Mrs Wentworth that morning, he had demonstrated nothing except his skill as a lady's hairdresser, he had canvassed to new customers, collected no money and another day had gone.

As he drove through the main street, buses were disgorging workers from the factory estate. They crowded in their hundreds and thousands through the steel barrier poles at the bus stops.

'Bloody sheep!' Albert muttered as he drove. 'Sheep in the pens waiting for the chopper! What have they done today?' Talking to himself gave him a feeling of superiority; utterance gave authenticity to a man's philosophy. You could agree with yourself and it sounded like two of you. 'Still,' he continued — slowing down for a mob on a pedestrian crossing — 'you can shear sheep. Big deal! That's right, mate, stare — you do the work, I get the lolly!' Tomorrow he would really get stuck in. . . .

'Albert!'

Albert heard the call, caught a glimpse of Cedric Mason standing by the gate of the playground at the school. Oh Christ! Albert thought. But he stopped and the schoolteacher came running up; a middle-aged man in a dirty macintosh holding a bulging shabby suitcase full of homework.

'Give us a lift, Albert?' he asked, stooping to the low window of the van.

'Yes, sir — Cedric — sure. Hop in! Welcome!'

'Sold my wife anything today?' the teacher asked when Albert had started up. 'One of your best clients I should think — our house is like a palace. It's a marvel how she manages, isn't it? Still, she's the organizer in our family. Nothing like a good marriage, Albert! Catch 'em while they're young and train 'em up. We all need organizing.'

'That's your washing machine in the back — taking it back for service,' Albert told him.

'What's the matter with it?' Cedric Mason asked, looking back into the van.

'Acid got into the bearings,' Albert said. 'That's all the sweat out of your shirts, sir — Cedric.'

The schoolteacher laughed. 'You can't work too hard. Keeps your mind off the state of the world. Besides, if you work hard you haven't got time to be ill. Remember what I used to tell you in standard six?'

'Long time ago, sir.'

'I expect it seems like it to you. There you are, you see — you've got older but I haven't, have I? Do I look forty-five?'

'Forty-five! No, sir!'

Cedric beamed at him. 'It surprises everybody — born nineteen-seventeen — '

'I remember, sir — same year as the Russian revolution, Ingrid Bergman, and Nancy Spain!'

The laughed together as they had in standard six.

'You've got to keep going, that's the secret, Albert.'

'Yes, sir — it's all go.'

'You take Marjorie — full of energy! Pops like a breakfast cereal all day long! Mind you, she's only twenty-seven.'

'She's always at it,' Albert said, his eyes on the road ahead.

'You're wasting your time there, you know, Albert.'

'Eh?' Albert exclaimed. He dare hardly look at his passenger who was staring at him, seriously concerned.

'On this job,' Cedric said.

'Oh,' Albert said.

'You shouldn't be a tally-boy. Tally-boys are ten a penny. There's no future in it. It's a transitory occupation. You're living on the sickness of the times — people living outside their income in a fool's paradise of plenty. They don't know it but they're going through the worst period of inflation in the history of the country.'

'Is that right?' Albert said.

'It won't last, thank God,' the schoolteacher said. 'The generation coming through school now will have different values — that's our job. It's the only place to start. I drum it into them. Work for what you get, pay for what you have — you ask Marjorie. Doesn't owe you anything now, does she?'

'She's clear up to date,' Albert said evasively.

'I educated her to start with,' the schoolteacher said. 'Of course, it's not easy. We all have to work it out in our own way. Pride of possession, that's what people don't have any more; I tell my class — the boy with an unbeatable conker in his pocket has got more to be proud of than the boy with an unpaid-for transistor radio.'

'I know what you mean,' Albert said.

And for the first time in their whole long acquaintance-ship as pupil and master, husband and wife's lover, Albert did know what he meant. Albert's greatest achievement in school was in having an undefeated conker. Albert had impregnated it with shellac, baked it, impregnated it again, and repeated the process over days and weeks — it was his greatest sustained effort and one which he would never surpass. The conker had finally become a dreadful thing; shellac, skin, and pith had merged and fused and polymerized until it was unnatured and harder and black-er and more uncrushable than granite.

Albert's conker had shattered hundreds of lesser conkers; it had subdued bullies, got him a place in the football team, won him a schoolboy's fortune in sweets and kind. The fearsome reputation of Albert's conker had spread to every school in the town and Albert had become a celebrity.

Moreover, it was Albert's conker which had given Albert a permanent taste for fame and acclaim and left him crippled by dissatisfaction and restlessness. Pride of possession! That's what was missing all right. You get this and you get that and you get the other — but it's never really yours.

Albert drove up a ramp into the petrol station and cut his motor. 'So long, then, sir.'

'Of course, it won't happen at once,' Cedric told him.

'What's that, sir?'

'Once we get right into the Common Market we're going to have to compete again. This country was always at its best with good strong competition — take the Spanish Main, take Hitler. War is competition, you know. We can work when we have to — once we can see the field!'

'That's true,' Albert said.

'Your dad was killed in France, wasn't he? I remember you used to do a job out of school hours helping to keep your mother — '

'I used to spend it all!' Albert said, growing red at this tribute. 'I never helped her much.'

'There'll be hard times again before they're good,' Cedric said. 'That's what I tell them. There'll be unemployment and poverty before we get any prosperity. But when it comes it'll be real prosperity. Not what we've got now, Albert — an artificial standard of living with everybody doing three jobs to keep up with it. That's not a healthy nation.'

'You're right,' Albert said.

'How old are you, Albert — twenty-two?'

'Twenty-four,' Albert said.

'There's still time,' his old master told him.

Albert looked at him.

'You were a bright scholar — good at English and maths when you put your mind to it. I didn't have any better start than you, Albert. I went to night school and studied through correspondence — you don't remember the old Bennett College? Let Me Be Your Father. I got an external B.Sc. with honours and won a grant to teachers' training college. You could do the same.'

'What me? A teacher?'

'Or an engineer or a scientist — they're the producers, Albert. They're what this country needs. Not tally-boys!'

'I thought I might have a go at the stage when I get the time — I've done a bit of singing.'

'Is that why you changed your name, Albert? Silly thing to do — insult to your father. Argyle isn't even spelt properly with an "e" — it's really a Scottish name. A place, a regiment, a football team!'

'I took it from Argyle Street — it was the closest I could get to the Palladium.'

'Silly chap,' Cedric told him. 'You're envying the wrong people. Actors, crooners, entertainers, strip-comic writers — they're not real, Albert, any more than tally-boys are. They're not giving anything, they're not achieving anything. At the end of a whole lifetime they haven't moved the clock forward by one minute. They live in the cracks and miss life altogether.'

'I couldn't be a scientist,' Albert said. 'I don't feel like a scientist.'

'You used to get top marks — remember how we measured the moisture content of grain?'

'What, the capacitive method in an oscillatory circuit?' Albert asked.

'There you are, you see — you haven't forgotten. Do you remember the dielectric constants of solids?'

'Not the figures,' Albert said.

'What's a pH unit?' the schoolmaster asked.

'Albert thought for a moment, then said: 'It's a measure of acidity and alkalinity directly proportional to fourteen times the logarithm of the ratio of disassociated hydrogen ions in an aqueous solution — '

'In grams per litre,' Cedric gave him.

Albert felt strangely proud. 'I didn't know I could remember that!'

'Well, it just shows. You could go on. It takes years of hard grind and doing without, but it's the only way if you really want to do something worth while with your life — '

'Cedric — get your finger out, mate!'

The schoolteacher scrambled out of the van, took an oil-stained overall off a peg and started getting into it. 'Filthy expression!' he said. Then he said: 'You bear it in mind, Albert!'

There came the blaring of a motor horn, 'Coming sir!' Cedric cried, running to fill the tank.

Albert watched him, shaking his head. 'I will,' he said. And as he drove away, he added, to himself: 'I dunno — you are a shit, Albert.' And a moment later he added again, comfortingly: 'But at least you know it. . . . '

'There's a man been here after you, Mr Argyle,' Hetty told him as Albert came into the shop.

'What another one?'

Jack Trevor Story

'This was a different one. I never seen him before. He wanted your private address but I told him, I said: "I am not allowed to divulge information about the staff!" — you know, like you told me to tell that girl and she began to break the place up. Any road up, he went away without another word.'

She whispered then, bending over the cash desk to him and pointing towards the back room: 'I was afraid he might bump into Jeff and he might tell him where you lived — I wouldn't put it past him!' Jeff came through and she raised her head, talking loudly: 'So if you'll just give me your figures for the day I can get totted up and toddle off home to me dear ones!'

'Wait a minute!' Albert had a disturbing thought about the visitor and dashed out of the shop.

'Where's he gone?' Jeff asked.

'Have you got anything to declare, Mr Jeffries?' Hetty asked.

'One Wondersew machine,' Jeff told her; he was still smarting. 'I left it on dem — chalk it up, will you, Hetty?'

Albert came back. 'It's still there.'

'What is?' Jeff asked him.

'My car. I've got an idea the HP bods are after it.'

'Haven't you had a letter terminating the agreement?' Jeff asked. 'They always send a letter once you go over three months without paying.'

'You don't have to tell me. I'm still paying off on the last car — if they take this one I'll be paying for two cars I haven't got. Have we got any of those polyvinyl car covers left?'

Hetty scanned her books: 'Twenty-four,' she said.

'Three,' Jeff told him. 'Over there.'

Hetty shrugged it off, got busy with pencil and rubber.

Albert found a cover and took it out to cover up his car and hide the number plate.

'Why didn't you get a letter?' Jeff asked him when he came back in. 'They always send a letter. If they haven't sent a letter they're not after it. Why go to all that trouble of covering it up? You can't put a plastic cover right over the bloody car every time you stop for ten minutes. If they haven't sent you a letter you're all right.'

'They don't know where I live,' Albert said. 'Why do you think I moved out of my last place?'

'I thought you run out on Treasure because she was expecting — '

'Why don't you knock it off?' Albert told him. 'I left to get away from letters and bailiffs and court orders — now you know. And if anybody wants to know where I live, you don't know. Okay? Christ, of course they've sent a letter by this time. The place was roof-high with bloody letters when I left — what d'you think?'

'I don't know all your bloody business,' Jeff said. 'You can't be in it any deeper than I am.' He drew Albert away from the cash desk. 'I got something to tell you —'

'Talking about Treasure, Mr Argyle,' Hetty called, 'did you get that washing machine from the Masons'?'

'In the van — tell Arnold to get it in, will you? I'm not going to strain my gut any more today.'

'There was this bloody cow of a woman,' Jeff told him. 'She was ugly. I swear she was really ugly — I wouldn't've touched her with yours let alone mine. . . . '

Mr Callendar came from his office wearing a navy-blue double-breasted suit. Lock up tonight, Hetty, will you — I've been invited to a cocktail party — '

'My, my, we're coming up, aren't we?' Hetty said.

'I don't know why you should say that. I often go to cocktail parties — I hold them meself. A man in my position is bound to get invited to cocktail parties. Where else do you think we business men talk business — ' He glanced round, then said: 'See that the boys all get away before you lock up. Good night, Hetty.'

'I've got a petition for you to sign,' Arnold told Hetty, coming down from the upper floor. 'Woodman spare that tree! What a day's work! Four orders and twenty-five signatures for a tree — did you tell Mr Callendar I lost the dem cleaner?'

'No. He was in a good mood. I didn't want to spoil

his evening.' She looked at the tree petition. 'What's this then?'

'Ah, never mind — I'm going to tear it up. Waste my time on a lot of old fogies — I should say so.'

'Let's have a look,' Albert said, coming back with Jeff trailing behind.

'It was a real confidence trick,' Jeff was saying.

'What d'you want to tear it up for?' Albert said to Arnold, reading the petition. 'It might be the only useful thing you ever get the chance to do in your whole mucky life.'

'You take it round, then,' Arnold said. And in case he was under any sort of misapprehension: 'They're all old dears — there's no crumpet, y'know.'

'I tell you what.' Albert turned to Hetty. 'Make out two more sheets.' He gave her the one to copy, then said to his colleagues: 'I'll lay a quid I get more signatures than you by six o'clock Friday night?'

'That's on,' Arnold said.

'I've got a good mind to report 'em to the police — they could get five years for a trick like that,' Jeff said broodingly.

Albert picked up the telephone receiver, dialled a number. 'Hello, darling — oh, can I speak to Miss Doris Masters, please . . . Doris? Remember me? Coffee bar this morning? . . . I know — you've been on my mind all day, dear. Wondered if you'd like a little drink somewhere this evening. . . . Wherever you like, I'll pick you up. . . .'

Jeff and Arnold exchanged a glance behind his back. Jeff put his thumb up.

Hetty was typing a heading on sheets of lined foolscap paper, using two fingers, laboriously:

We, the undersigned, do hereby register our strong disapproval at the intended destruction of the old sycamore tree in Cheveley Square. This tree has great sentimental value to the elderly residents and we petition the council to reconsider its decision, save the tree and earn the heartfelt gratitude of the community.

Having written, read, and inwardly digested this, Hetty looked up at the tally-boys in sheer disbelief, suspecting a joke.

10

'AND what's the little lady drinking? What are you having, my dear?' Major Simpkins was patting Joyce Corby's hand in a corner of the room. 'They don't look after you, do they? If you were mine, I'd look after you — by golly, yes! Wish I was six months younger, what?'

Joyce was staring across the room at her husband, who was talking to Mr Callendar, Mr Wisbech, a bank manager, Mr Solly Cowells who owned the biggest department store in town, and a woman he had brought with him but had not introduced. Joyce's eyes had not left her husband since he had arrived home. She was trying, quite simply, to reconcile him — Reggie, the husband she thought she knew — with the voice from that bathroom.

'What?' she said to the elderly military strategist.

'You look lovely,' he said. 'Ravishing, my dear.'

'Thank you.'

'And what's the rest of this delightful flat like, eh?' said the major, opening a bedroom door and easing her through. 'We shan't be missed, shall we? Keep talking. Rhubarb, rhubarb, rhubarb. Oh yes, lovely room. Lovely. Looks south.'

'Reggie!' Joyce called, from behind the gentleman's bulk as he bulldozed her into the bedroom.

The woman who had arrived with Mr Cowells came across, talking to the bank manager with with one interested eye on the open bedroom door.

'Mind you,' she was saying, 'I always know what kind of people are living in any house, just by looking at it. They may take big houses, but they remain vulgarly working-class — did you call, Mrs Corby?'

'Just taking a look round — lovely place, don't you

think so, Mrs — er — um?' said the Major.

'I was just saying to Mr Wisbech, so many of our best houses and flats are falling into the hands of the working class — such a pity!'

The rest of the party eased across the threshold of the bedroom, which was Reggie's.

'And look at that divine headboard,' said Mr Cowell's lady friend. 'It's a work of art! It really is.'

'And why not?' Major Simkins said. 'Reggie's going to be chairman of the council before long, you see.'

Reggie laughed, modestly. 'I have to get elected first.'

'I'll get you there,' said the major. 'Tactics, old boy!' He smiled down at Joyce. 'I'm a master of tactics. A bit of money, a bit of influence — when you haven't got party funds then you need a few good friends, eh?'

'And another thing that always gives them away is their windows,' said the woman to Mr Wisbech. 'You don't have to meet the people, just look at the bedroom windows. The working class, no matter what kind of mansion they may be in, always block out their windows with the ugly back of a dressing-table —.'

'That's right,' Mr Wisbech said. 'That's perfectly true.'

'They prefer themselves to the view or the daylight,' the woman said. 'Complete lack of aesthetic feeling, you see — no amount of money will give them that.'

'And they always vote Conservative,' said Mr Wisbech. 'It's a kind of defence, I suppose. Not that class bothers me, mind you — it's a completely classless society these days.'

'Completely!' his companion echoed. Then she cleared her throat. Everybody was staring at the Corby dressing-table which Joyce had arranged with its back to the window, blocking the view.

'Yes, well, how about letting me fill you up?' Reggie said. He had darted a disgusted look at his wife who had turned scarlet.

'That's the idea!' exclaimed Major Simpkins. 'Back to the pump!'

But he stood his ground, holding his hostess's arm

until the others had gone back into the lounge. Then he went over and closed the door.

'Lot of nincompoops, you know, my dear. My dressing-table's got its back to the window — wouldn't have it any other way.'

'It never occurred to me before,' Joyce said. 'I'll move it tomorrow.'

'You don't want to do that — be an individualist. A beautiful gal like you can have anything the way she wants it.' He took her glass and placed it beside his own on the offending dressing-table. 'Now let's look at you!' He squeezed her close. 'My word, what a stunner you are!'

'Major Simpkins!' she exclaimed.

In the mirror, as she stood thus embraced, unable to move, she saw the door open and Reggie look in.

'Ooooops!' he said. 'So sorry, Major — don't let me interrupt.' And he closed the door firmly on them.

'Splendid chap, your husband,' muttered the Major, thickly, kissing her all over her face as she tried to avoid him. 'Knows how to make his signals!'

'What are you doing!' Joyce exclaimed.

'Let's get over to the bed, eh — too old for knee tremblers these days — '

Joyce Corby brought her knee up, sharply. The major collapsed back on to the bed, holding himself, blue in the face, gasping and groaning.

'Can I get you a drink?' she asked, going to the door and flinging it open. 'I think Major Simpkins has had a bit of an attack,' she said to the lounge at large.

They all turned towards her, Reggie's face white as a daisy in a bed of poppies. Instinctively he knew that she had let him down again.

In a house in Cavendish Street, Mr and Mrs Wentworth were in bed together.

'And what sort of a day have you had?' he asked.

Coral wriggled closer to him, feeling a little conscience-stricken. 'I did a bit of shopping. What sort of day have you had, dear?'

'Lot of trouble with the management.'

'Oh, never mind. Don't worry about it,' Coral told him.

'I'm not at the moment,' he said.

'You do your job and don't get mixed up in it,' she advised. 'We don't want any strikes — not now we're getting straight.

'There won't be any strikes, darling.'

'I'm glad,' she said.

We're going to work to rule,' he said.

'Oh. What does that mean?'

'Just cut out overtime for a bit — what's the matter, darling?'

'But we've budgeted on overtime!'

'Well, don't let's worry about it now. Darling . . . Darling. Coral.' There was no reply. 'Have you lost interest? Darling? Never mind,' he said. 'Just keep still.'

Outside the house where he lived Albert was fed up. It had been another of those evenings. It had again cost him money that wasn't his, but this time he had managed to get the girl back with him — only to find that the light in his room was on, the curtains drawn. Jeff or Arnold was in possession.

'We had this funny old schoolmistress, Miss Thanet,' the girl was saying. 'She had these stuffed birds. They used to give me the creeps! She tried to make us wear shorts for gym, but I wouldn't and she didn't half go on. That was where I met Hilda — I told you about Hilda — who married John, you remember, the parson's son who worked on the roads? I saw John's friend Ken only last week — he was very keen on me, I don't know why — but he didn't see me. I was coming down Butterhall Street — you know where Cranby's is? Well, I saw him looking into this shop window and I crossed over, see? Well, when I got to the end of the street — I didn't turn back, mind you — he must have seen me because as I turned up to the office he came hurrying along. I pretended I hadn't

seen him and went in. The girls were killing themselves —
they were looking out of the window and they told me
afterwards — where are you going?'

'I'm driving you home,' Albert said.

It was never, never worth it.

At one o'clock he let himself into his bed-sitting-room.
There were dirty cups and saucers, bottles and glasses
still out, the divan cover half off showing a patched
mattress. Albert lay down on the divan, lit a cigarette,
stared at the ceiling. Bloody tally-boys; they had no
respect for anything or anybody. On the ceiling little
silver paper egg-cups had been tossed up and gobstuck.
God knows what he would find in the lavatory.

Albert turned on his side, suddenly, as though to hide
his face from the empty, smoke-soured room, and pulled
a cushion towards him.

'Treasure,' he said, 'why do you hate me?'

Part Two

NEVER JAM TOMORROW

11

AS Albert ran down the stairs the next morning the black man came out of his room.

'Mr Argyle?'

'That's me, Sambo.' Albert's friendly grin took away the impertinence. He noticed a Negro woman just inside the door and a child sitting at a breakfast table, staring and listening.

'Could I have a word with you?' the Negro asked. 'My name is Russel — Joe Russel. It's about last night.'

'Oh. You got some noise from my place?'

'I don't want you to think I'm the complaining kind of neighbour as I've just moved in, but — '

'I can guess — it wasn't me, you know,' Albert said. 'What were they up to?'

Joe Russel shook his head in wonderment. 'Man! There was some kind of I-don't-know-what going on — shrieking and banging and girls and fellows on the stairs undressed — well, I don't want to complain, but — '

'It won't happen again, Mr Russel! I give you my word.'

'You see, I've got a family to consider and my kid — he was in and out of bed — well, somebody swore at him — mind you, I think they were drunk, but you know — well, we can't afford trouble and if anybody's going to complain I've got to get my complaint in first — do you understand that, Mr Argyle?'

'Sure, sure — it won't happen again.'

'That's the position we're in — but mind you, we like it here, only last night my wife was frightened we'd got into the wrong house — we have to be careful — and she wanted me to go and see the landlord this morning but I'd rather have a word with you first — do you understand?'

'It won't happen again,' Albert told him. 'I'd already decided that when I saw the mess they left — you do somebody a favour and that's what happens. They're not coming here any more. I'd already decided — as a matter of fact I'm getting married myself pretty soon.'

'Well, congratulations!' Joe Russel said. His wife was smiling now round the door, the black child was eating again.

Albert said: 'Thanks.'

'Perhaps you'd like the wife to clear up for you?' Joe Russel said. 'She'd be happy to clean the place up for you.'

'Well that's good of you — ' Albert was feeling in his pocket.

'No money!' the Negro exclaimed. 'I didn't mean that — you just leave the key.'

'Well thanks,' Albert said. 'The key's under the carpet outside my door — it's very good of you. Much obliged. See you!'

Albert was glad to get away. When people started behaving like human beings he ran out of patter. Besides — who was getting married? You could take consumer identification too far. And however he felt last night, Albert was his own man again this morning. No targets today. Just get stuck in. If he didn't make any appointments with himself then he didn't fail to keep them; if he didn't make any promises to himself, he didn't break them.

He had parked the car two streets away to be on the safe side, and it was shrouded in the polyvinyl cover. He took a quick look round before taking it off. He didn't want to lose this one. What else did he get out of life for all the work he did and the running around and worrying? The car, cigarettes, the occasional girl.

He drove quickly away, feeling like a thief.

The Corbys were having breakfast.

'You could have played him along a little,' Reggie said. 'He doesn't mean any harm.'

'I got frightened,' Joyce said. 'You don't know what he did. He touched me — you know where.'

'Don't be vulgar!' her husband said.

'Perhaps you wouldn't mind if I went with him,' Joyce said, 'as long as he got you on the council.'

'That hardly needs an answer,' Reggie said, coldly. 'You have a typically working-class view of that sort of thing.'

'You mean I think it's wrong when you're not married?' Joyce said.

'I mean it's something one doesn't discuss at the breakfast table.'

Joyce picked at her bacon. 'Would you go with anybody else?'

'Certainly not. Not if it meant anything.'

'Oh, I see. It's all right if it doesn't mean anything?'

'It's all right for men, I suppose. Not really important. For women it's different.' He looked at her. 'Shall we talk about something else?'

Joyce said: 'That's a typically universal view — amongst men!'

He said: 'Have you got a spare pound out of the housekeeping, dear? I ran out yesterday — had an expensive client to entertain. I'll get it back out of petty cash.'

'Who was she?' Joyce asked.

'Who said it was a she? Anyway, have you or haven't you?'

'Did you take her out to lunch?' Joyce asked.

'No. Drinks — and so on. I'll give it to you back tonight.'

'How much did it cost you?'

'About three pounds.'

'Was it successful?' Joyce asked.

'What d'you mean?'

'Well, did she do whatever you wanted her to do?'

'She didn't take the flat, if that's what you mean. Too small for her — Lady Renwick, you've heard me speak of her. President of the Dog Club. She's interested in my proposal for dog-troughs in the town. It may help me to get in. She thought it was an excellent idea to offer the voters something that would appeal to the heart rather than the pocket. She said I was an idealist.'

Joyce waited for more, interestedly. 'What did she look like? I mean, what is she like? Pretty?'

'Good heavens no — raddled old thing. Stinks of dogs.'

'I haven't got a pound to spare,' Joyce said. 'Not even ten bob.' If he could invent the conversation, why not a less revolting woman?

'Ten shillings!' Her husband corrected. 'I don't know what you do with it.'

'Funny you should say that,' Joyce said. 'I've got a list made out.'

Reggie stopped eating. 'I've got to go,' he said.

'If you go now,' Joyce said, 'I shan't be here when you come back!'

It was their first quarrel and it was a big one, though for the first time Reggie took the minor role of listener. He learned what he did with his money and what she had to do to get it back. He discovered how many things in their home were still unpaid for. He found out what he thought of his mother. She spoke steadily for a quarter of an hour and although she was not always grammatically correct she was graphic, fluent, and frighteningly articulate. He could either go, leaving her the flat and its contents, most of which she was paying for, and making her a suitable allowance; or he could stay on her terms.

'What terms?' he asked, nervously.

'I want a baby and one of those new thirty-guinea prams to take in the park,' she said. 'I don't care if it's your baby or Major Simpkins's, if that's of any help to you, but — '

'I'll stay,' Reggie said. 'But don't tell mother!' Now that the cards were on the table he tried to get his money back.

'No,' Joyce told him. 'I've promised it to Mr Argyle.'

Reggie went. Joyce collapsed, laughing, on the Regency settee. He's not the only one who knows how to make his signals, she was thinking. And if you can't fight 'em, join 'em. On this thought she went into the bedroom and started moving the dressing-table away from the window. It was heavy and she had to struggle with it, one end at a time. Whatever else we are, she thought, let us not be working-class. With the dressing-table out of the way she opened the big window and gazed at the unaccustomed view. Perhaps Mr Argyle would give her a baby? Reggie would never know and never care. She started singing. Honest to God — what she had been missing! Ethics could be fun once you knew what they were.

She took a dartboard from under her bed and hanging it on the wall she started playing. That was another thing he didn't know about.

On a mischievous impulse she took one of the darts into the lounge and aimed it at the painting of the horse.

In a semi-detached house at Fenton Park, one of the middle-bracket owner-occupier estates, a plump, homely girl was making porridge when Albert came in the back door. She held the saucepan at arm's length while he cuddled and kissed her.

'You've got nothing underneath again, you naughty mother!'

'I haven't had time!'

'Mummy!' came a cry from the next room.

'Go and keep 'em quiet, love,' she told him. 'There's some tea poured out.'

'You smell warm and clean and milky,' Albert told her.

He went through into the living-room. Four young children were round the table, one in a baby's high chair. There was a clamour of welcome from them. Albert gave them a sweet each to spoil their breakfast, then looked at the tea tray.

'Where's mine, Grace?' he called.

'He's on the pottie,' came the reply.

A moment later she came in with the porridge and the small boy who was a little older than the washing

Live Now, Pay Later 95

machine.

'How long have you worn that shirt?' Grace asked as they sat with the children, Albert feeding his son, drinking tea. 'You'd better let me have it — you can have a clean one of Fred's.'

'I think this is Fred's,' Albert said. 'How is he?'

'He's fine,' Grace told him. 'Did I tell you he's just had another rise? They think a lot of him at Oggles.'

'They should. He's a good mechanic.'

'He misses you,' Grace told Albert. 'He keeps asking when you're going to bring Treasure round for a game of Monopoly again. I thought it best not to tell him you weren't with her any more. Have you seen her? I wonder how she's getting on?'

'What about another cup?' Albert said.

She poured him a second cup. 'Fred liked Treasure. You know what he always said? She is just right for Albert! Just what he needs! Somebody to keep his feet on the ground! I wish you'd make up, Albert. I mean, she must've got over it by this time. That stuff worked, didn't it? In the end.'

'Everything worked at once,' Albert said.

Grace sighed her sympathy. 'I know — you've got to be careful when you're single. Still, you looked a lot better then — are you eating enough?' Then she said: 'Did she know about — him?' She nodded to the child on Albert's lap.

'What d'you think? She knew about everything. She knew what I was thinking before I thought it.'

Grace laughed. 'Well, I suppose that's what Fred meant. It's nice to have somebody you don't have to fool — then you don't have to fool yourself, do you?'

'It's like having an affair with your own conscience,' Albert said.

'What's an affair, mummy?' asked a boy of five.

'Wait till you start school, matey,' Albert told him.

Grace laughed with him. Later he changed his shirt in the kitchen and she gave him a clean ironed handkerchief for his top pocket. He cuddled her again.

Jack Trevor Story

'What's the matter, Albert?'

'Nothing. I just need cuddling.'

'I wish you weren't always wracking around, Albert. I think about you. I wish you were settled.'

'You haven't changed your mind, have you, Grace?'

'No, dear. It wouldn't be right. It was right once. It wouldn't be right any more. I don't need it now. I've got all I want. You don't know what that's like, do you?'

'I'm only twenty-four, Grace.'

'You seem older. You seem a lot older, sometimes.'

'I feel it,' Albert said. 'Time I got a partnership and told other people what to do.'

'You'll never get a partnership, Albert. You'll never do any more than talk about getting on. You don't want to get on. You don't want responsibility.'

'You sound like Treasure,' he said. Then he said: 'I've got my hand on your navel.'

'Feel better now?' she said. 'Come on — let me give you some money.'

'Could you pay a few weeks in advance, Grace — I'm a bit short?'

'Yes, of course — you can have five pounds and finish off the carpet shampooer.'

'Would you like something else?' he asked. 'I've got the catalogue outside.'

'If I start looking at that I'll never get any work done — leave it with me, I'll see if there's anything Fred wants. . . . '

He kissed her again, fondly, took the money, called a farewell to the children. Grace followed him out onto the garden path, looking at the sky.

'What's it going to do?'

'Take care of yourself,' Albert said.

'You take care of yourself, Albert.'

'I nearly forgot,' he said. 'Will you sign this petition to save an old tree?'

She read it, then put the sheet of paper against the doorpost and signed it with his biro.

'You're getting soft-hearted, aren't you?' she asked.

'Don't be daft — I've got a quid on who'll get the most signatures. Treasure would've known that!'

She smiled after him as he got in the van, then remembered the catalogue. 'Albert!' She waved. 'What about the catalogue?'

Albert waved back, putting the money into his pocket as he drove away.

Grace smiled to herself as she went in; Albert got all he wanted and went. Treasure would know that too. He couldn't help it. That's the way he was. But he still loved you in his own selfish way. Of course, it would never do to marry him. No doubt that's what had finished Treasure. In the end a woman always wants a marriage.

12

GRACE had relaxed Albert and lightened his spirits; to get the essence of a woman you didn't have to make love to her always. The love between them was implicit and unfiery, like ever-warm ashes from an old blaze. There was mother, mistress, and wife in what she gave him without going to bed — though he was still ready, for she had a climax in every touch.

Grace, surrounded by her children, seemed always warm and clean and naked underneath as though recently bathed and glowing with the milky vapours of clean warm flesh, and ready for another confinement. What she gave birth to in his heart and loins flowed in through his hands each time he touched her. 'I've got my hand on your navel,' he had told her. It was natural and elemental; somehow she seemed to expect it and accept it. She was calm, soothing, and good for him. She wanted him to have all that he could get from her, to make the best, moistest, and most sensuous contact he could, without breaking any more rules or hurting any more people.

Grace was contented within herself and she cared for him and for the child and she was happy to release him from all responsibility except that of taking care of himself. Take care of yourself was a polite cliché to all except those who loved and then it was a sacred responsibility. Albert was happy because he was loved; it wasn't Treasure, but it was something.

By eleven o'clock he had made fifteen calls and collected thirty-three pounds ten shillings. It wasn't his money, but it bulked in his inside breast-pocket and he was rich. Now he could set himself a target; he would make it, say, fifty pounds.

'You shouldn't have done that,' he told himself as he drove across town. 'You said no targets. You silly old bugger.'

And supposing the child in Grace's home was what Treasure had seen when she pulled the chain in the cinema lavatory. Wouldn't that make her hate him forever? The picture was getting more horrifyingly clear each time he thought about it. He was seeing it through Treasure's eyes.

'Let's celebrate?' he'd said when she crawled back into the balcony seat and whispered it to him.

'You bastard,' she had said, quietly, her eyes on the screen. 'You wicked bastard.'

Even then she had not cried.

To re-establish his self-confidence he decided to tackle some of the tough ones, get a few of the arrears in. At twenty-three Latimer Road he banged on the front door, then ran quickly around to the back just as the lady of the house was creeping out with a shopping basket.

'Hello!' she said. 'I wondered if I heard somebody knocking or if it was the pipes — could you leave it this week?'

'I left it last week and the week before,' Albert said, scanning his book. 'Can't let it go on any longer. Sorry, Mrs Kelly.'

The woman took her purse out of her shopping basket and gave him a pound note which he recorded. 'Ta very much, dear — can I give you a lift down to the shops?'

'Not now,' she said, throwing the empty purse back into the basket.

Farther along the road the opposition was stiffer. Albert had to get tough.

'Either you give me something or I'll have to take back the cleaner — suit yourself.'

'You wait a week and like it,' the woman said.

She closed the door on him. Albert didn't go.

'Mrs Fordyce!' he called. 'Mrs Fordyce!' He banged the door. 'Are you going to give me that cleaner or do I have to fetch a policeman?'

The door opened again and the woman glared at him, livid with anger, looking first one way then the other. 'Do you want the whole street to hear?'

'Yes, dear,' Albert said.

'I can give you ten shillings — and that's all!'

'A pound,' Albert said.

She gave him the money; he put it into his book.

'You can be really nasty, can't you, Mr Argyle?' she said.

'I'm in a nasty mood,' Albert told her.

I'll re-possess something today, he promised himself; he re-possessed more things than either of the other tally-boys. It took moral courage, and physical courage, sometimes. Callendar depended on Albert to deal with awkward customers.

'If they won't pay, git the goods out of the 'ouse!' was his alternative war-cry.

'I always know when you're hating yourself,' Treasure would tell him. 'You take it out on other people.'

'Balls!' Albert said, getting back into his van, slamming the door.

Outside a house in The Avenue, Albert opened the back doors of his van and cleared a space. He felt sure they wouldn't have the money; he didn't want the money.

'I've called for the guitar,' he told the woman who answered the door.

'Peter's guitar?' she said.

'No, our guitar, Mrs Barnwell. He's had it two months

without making a payment — '

'I'm afraid you can't take it — '

'Has he left the four pounds?' Albert asked.

'No, but — '

'Then I'm taking it,' Albert said. 'If he likes to come down to the warehouse with the money he can have it back.'

'It's not here,' she said.

'Has he sold it? He'll go to prison if he's sold it.'

'Of course he hasn't sold it — he's learned to play it. He's very good!'

'I'm glad,' Albert said. 'But we're not the musicians' benevolent society — will you get it for me, please?'

'He took it with him, this morning — on his scooter.'

'To work?' Albert said.

'All right, if you don't believe me — come in. Come and look for it! I'm not going to stand here and be insulted — I shall tell my husband about this. You're very rude. I know your sort — go around bullying women when their husbands are at work. It's you that ought to go to prison!'

'Well let me come in, then,' Albert said. 'I'm at work too, you know.'

He went in.

'This is his room,' the woman said. 'That's where he keeps it.'

Albert looked around the bedroom without finding a guitar.

'What about the other rooms?'

She took him all over the house. He looked into everything big enough to hide a guitar, including the gas oven, which wasn't.

'All right — where is it?' Albert said when they were back in the front hall.

'He took it to work with him. He's going straight on to a jazz party tonight in Beachfield Road.'

'Then why didn't you say that in the beginning?'

'I just wanted to see how objectionable you could be,' the woman said.

'What number Beachfield Road?'

'I don't know and I don't care — now do you mind going?'

'You could do with some new stair carpet,' Albert said. 'Would you like our catalogue?'

'What!' she exclaimed.

'And that television's about a hundred years old,' Albert told her. 'You want a new slim-line, madam.'

'It works perfectly!'

'I know — those old sets do.' Albert said. 'It's those old sets that are putting the manufacturers out of business.'

The woman suddenly laughed.

'You think about it,' Albert said, and he produced the petition. 'Would you like to sign this for me?'

She read it. 'You've got a nerve!'

'It's not just a tree,' he told her as she signed. 'They're chopping down all the old people.'

He slammed the back doors of his van on a lighter note — he had insulted her, searched her house, got her signature and left her laughing — he would probably get an order from her before very long.

'It's a gift, Albert,' he congratulated himself as he drove away.

By one o'clock he had collected forty-seven pounds; could he make his target of fifty before lunch and break all records? He sat in his van in a side-street, smoking a well-earned cigarette and scanning the list of customers. A girl walked past and he only whistled her. He could be strong. Especially when they scowled at him. But automatically his eyes searched for names which would smile at him and cancel out the scowl. Mrs Corby! If she hadn't any money she might give him lunch. Anyway, he would cheer her up if she needed it.

He started the motor, drove away.

Money? Lunch? Cheer her up? Who was he fooling? Write a letter for her — ah, there's an excuse he'd forgotten because it involved doing something. He was going to see Mrs Corby again from the moment she had stood there in that slim black dress with her hair high and looking tearful.

'Then why didn't I do it yesterday?' he asked himself.

That was the groundwork, Albert. We know that, don't we?

He was talking to Treasure again.

Joyce Corby was in the bathroom rinsing a shampoo out of her hair when the doorbell sounded.

'Coming!' she called.

She groped around for the towel and remembered that she had left it on the dressing table. She went out of the bathroom with her eyes closed, crossed the bedroom to where the dressing-table used to be. As she groped in front of her the bell sounded again.

'Coming!' she called.

Her knees struck the wall and she fell headlong across the windowsill; she opened her eyes and as they smarted with the soap she clutched for a hold with her wet hands. Most of her weight was out of the window.

'Oh my gawd! God!'

They were her last words.

There was a moment when she was holding and a moment when her fingers were slipping. As she fell out of the window, she screamed.

Albert, outside the flat door, heard the scream and the thump of her body on the ground without knowing what it was or where it came from. He rang the bell again, then tried the door handle; the door opened and he went into the flat.

'Mrs Corby? Are you there? It's me.'

He crossed the lounge and went through the open bedroom door. He looked from the open window to the open bathroom door and then to the towel lying on the dressing-table. That's a funny place to put a dressing-table, he thought. He went back into the lounge, then looked in the other bedroom. She was out, but she couldn't be far away. On the other hand she was sufficiently disorganized to have left the place open. He then saw her handbag lying on one of the Regency chairs.

Albert picked up the handbag. She had said that she

might have his money today. He opened it and took out three pound notes. He put them in his pocket with the rest and marked up the book. While he was doing this he heard a woman's frightened voice calling.

'Mrs Corby! Are you all right?'

The voice seemed to be coming from the bedroom and he went in. The calling drew him to the window and he looked out.

'Young man!' the voice came again. 'What's happened to Mrs Corby?'

He looked up and found Mrs Jenkins' frightened face gazing down at him from a window above.

'Did she fall?'

Now Albert looked down and saw the figure motionless and spreadeagled on the paved terrace below. He stared down blankly for a moment, not understanding. Then the sounds he had heard came back to him. He shouted up to the woman above: 'Don't be bloody silly – phone the ambulance!'

He rushed out of the room. It was her calling – Mrs Corby – when he rang the bell. It suddenly fitted into a terrifying pattern; the calls, the scream, the thump. It had hardly registered at the time; it could have been a radio or noises from another flat.

Albert jumped most of the stairs, raced across the vestibule and out round the side of the block. He was hoping somebody would get to her before he did. He knew nothing about first-aid. Accidents frightened him.

There was no blood. He went down on his knees beside her. She was lying half on her side, her face up, eyes closed. He listened for signs of breathing. She was all wet.

'Mrs Corby!' he said.

He pulled the bathrobe away from her throat – she was naked. Must have been having a bath, he thought.

'I've telephoned – they're coming!' The voice came from above and he looked up. 'The police as well!' Mrs Jenkins called.

'Bring some water!' Albert called. 'Bring some brandy!'

Mrs Jenkins was staring at him with frightened eyes.

Jack Trevor Story

She withdrew from the window, crossed the room and locked her door, drawing both bolts.

When the ambulance men arrived with a doctor Albert was blowing into the girl's mouth; he had read about it somewhere and it was all he could think of. He watched the doctor take over. People from nearby had been drawn by the arrival of the ambulance, an old lady with a small dog, a boy on a tricycle, two window cleaners. At-home-in-the-middle-of-the-day people; incidents like this dropped like a bomb into their unbusy world.

'I'm afraid she's dead,' the doctor told Albert. 'I'm sorry. Is she your . . . ?'

'Mrs Corby,' Albert said. 'One of my customers. She fell. She must have fallen. I don't know.'

'You'd better sit down,' the doctor said.

Albert sat on the front steps of the block of flats, watching the draped body being carried into the ambulance. A police car stopped and several policemen alighted from it. Mrs Jenkins now appeared out of the flats and ran past Albert towards the policemen.

'I heard her scream!' he heard her exclaim.

Albert felt weak, sick, empty. He had liked her. He had felt sorry for her. He really had. Yesterday he had combed her hair, now she was dead; a stranger again. He had not even known her first name.

'Is this the gentleman, madam?' A policeman was bringing Mrs Jenkins back to the flats. She nodded, staring at Albert without speaking, still with that shocked, frightened look.

'Will you come inside, sir?' the man said.

'Yes, sure.' Albert stood up.

'Hello, Albert,' one of the policemen said.

Albert was grateful to see a constable he knew. 'Hello, Sid — this is a rotten business, isn't it — ' Suddenly, without warning, he was sick. He had tasted toothpaste from the unbreathing mouth.

'Put your head down there, mate,' the constable said, holding Albert's shoulders.

As he retched by the door into the shrubbery he heard

the voices as if a great crowd was gathering.

'He did his best for her,' came the doctor's voice. 'But it was too late.'

'Did you know her well?' a police sergeant asked.

Albert felt the question was directed at him. 'No. She was a customer.'

'What's her full name?'

'I don't know,' Albert said. 'Mrs Corby. That's all I know.'

'Well I only said what I thought,' came Mrs Jenkins' voice from a great distance. 'And if it isn't blood it must be lipstick!'

'You should be careful,' came the sergeant's voice.

'Better, mate?' asked the constable.

Albert stood up, wiping his mouth. 'Thanks, Sid.'

They went inside, leaving a group on the pavement.

'I'm sure I'm wrong, superintendent. I'm sorry I mentioned it. I wouldn't like him to get to hear.'

Mrs Jenkins was in her sitting-room talking to Detective Superintendent Collins of the county C.I.D.

'It was just the way it looked to me. I saw him go into the flat with her yesterday afternoon and then she saw him off wearing a different dress — and their conversation was very familiar. Well, that was yesterday. Then today I heard her scream and when I looked out of the window she was lying on the terrace. The next moment he put his head out of the window and looked up at me. He seemed very frightened and he spoke to me roughly — but of course I can see now that he could be perfectly innocent. I'm sure he is. You won't say I saw anything, will you, superintendent? Once he knew my life wouldn't be worth twopence!'

'Did you like Mrs Corby?' the detective asked.

'Well, I never had much to do with her — none of us did in the block. She was very working-class for our neighbourhood.'

'I see.'

'Not that that means anything these days, of course.'

Jack Trevor Story

'Well that'll be all, thank you, madam. We shall want you to give evidence at the inquest.'

'Oh dear — shall I have to tell them everything? I mean — will *he* be there? I suppose I can have police protection?'

'It's people like us who want protecting from people like them,' the superintendent told his subordinate officer as they drove back to the police station. There wasn't a man on the force in the town who had passed his eleven-plus or its equivalent.

'It's not fair on Argyle,' the sergeant said. 'He ought to have her up for libel.'

'I don't think she'll say any more. I let her see it wasn't popular. Anyway, she's too scared.'

Later Albert made a statement to the superintendent at the police station. In the statement room, besides the superintendent, there was the sergeant, two constables, including the one called Sid whom Albert knew, and a woman police constable. Sid had provided Albert with tea, biscuits, and cigarettes.

'It's quite true,' Albert said. 'I was there nearly an hour, yesterday. I helped her choose a dress for this party.'

'That was decent of you,' the superintendent said.

The woman police constable, who was busy writing, now looked round at the men.

'Then I gave her a new hair-style,' Albert said.

'I bet she was pleased,' the sergeant said.

'And then I helped her with her accounts — she was very worried about some debts.'

'Was she now?' the superintendent said. 'That's interesting. Wait a bit and we'll take that down.' He turned to the sergeant. 'Write that bit down, it might be pertinent. Very worried about debts. That's a good bit.' He turned to Albert. 'Would you like some more tea?'

Albert accepted another cup of tea and told them what he had learned and what he had, since Mrs Corby's death, conjectured about the marriage.

'He kept her short of money,' Albert said.

'I'm not surprised,' the superintendent said. 'We'll get that down. Anything else?'

'He kept pulling her up about the way she spoke and so on,' Albert said. 'I think he made her feel inferior.'

'Isn't it marvellous!' the superintendent said. 'And yet that old bitch liked him all right. He's the right class. Him and his Bentley.'

A young constable looked in. 'Mr Corby's here, sir.'

'Is he? Is he now?' the superintendent said. 'Has he done the identification?'

'Yes, super.'

'Well now he can wait till I've finished with Mr Argyle, can't he?' the superintendent said. 'Inferior!' He turned to Albert: 'And you say that lipstick was on your shirt before you called at the dead woman's flat?'

'Yes, I got that at an earlier call,' Albert said.

'Yes, well, we'll scrub round that, shall we? Miss that bit out, Sergeant. That's not pertinent.'

The woman police constable sighed and continued with her work.

As Albert went out of the superintendent's office, Reginald Corby got up from a chair and intercepted him. They had met briefly in the police station entrance as Albert was coming in and Reggie was going to the mortuary.

'Mr Argyle — could I have a private word with you?' Reggie asked.

'What about?' Albert asked.

'Did she say anything before she died? My wife?'

'What sort of thing?'

'Anything? Did she speak?' He broke off as the constable beckoned him. 'Just a minute, officer!' Then softly to Albert: 'Did she?'

The slight interruption had given Albert time to hate Corby. 'As a matter of fact she did,' Albert said.

'What did she say?' Reggie whispered. 'Was it about me?'

Albert said: 'She said: "He drove me to it!" They were her last words, "He drove me to it!" '

Reggie turned pale. 'Have you told the police?'

'No,' Albert said. 'It slipped my mind till you mentioned it.'

'Don't tell them, will you? I mean, it can only make it worse. After all, it was an accident. Must have been. You won't tell them, will you, Mr Argyle?'

'Not unless they ask me,' Albert said.

'The coroner will ask you. Bound to.'

'Well, I can't falsify evidence, can I?' Albert said.

'You work for Teddy Callendar, don't you?' Reggie said. 'He's a great friend of mine. I'm negotiating a big deal for him.'

'What's that got to do with it?' Albert said.

'Come along, sir,' the constable called.

Reggie watched Albert go out of the police station. He drove me to it! My God, that's just the sort of cliché she would go out on. He could see it in the papers.

The early edition of the local evening paper carried a full-length picture of Joyce Corby wearing a bikini bathing suit, a crown, and the 'Miss Agricultural Tractors 1959' sash across her middle. 'Ex-Beauty Queen dies in fall from bedroom — local man's heroic life-saving attempt' was the heading. And opposite was a head-and-shoulders photograph of Albert taken on the steps of the police station alongside a picture of Corby.

'Oh, brother — what a figure!' Jeff was saying as they all looked at the paper spread on the counter. 'Look at those child-bearing hips. Don't tell me you weren't knocking it, Albert!'

'Oh, Mr Jefferies!' Hetty exclaimed.

Arnold said: 'You could've had half my territory for that, Albert.'

Albert looked at his colleague in disgust. 'If you rotted I wouldn't use you for manure,' he told them. 'No bloody feelings. You're lower than animals, you are. She's dead, in case you've forgotten.'

Arnold said: 'She looks alive there.'

'The lifefulness is terrific!' Jeff said.

'And I don't want you picking your nose over my carpet any more,' Albert said to Arnold. He looked at

Jeff: 'I've had complaints about your orgy last night — it's all over, finished. You owe me a quid each.'

'You go and fart for it,' Jeff told him.

Arnold said: 'You're going to owe me a quid each this time tomorrow — how many signatures have you got?'

The three of them buried their animosities while they compared the petitions for the tree. Hetty took the newspaper back to her desk.

'You lousy bugger, Jeff! You've been forging those signatures! Two hundred and fifty my arse! That's your left-handed writing you use to bump up your sales contracts!'

'Psst!' Hetty called. She pointed to Mr Callendar's office.

In his office Mr Callendar was also studying the front page of the paper. 'Heroes! ! Such heroes!' he muttered.

'Albert!' he called.

'Now see what you've done!' Jeff said.

Albert went into the office.

'Close the door, Albert. Sit down. Can you spare a moment? It's been a very 'arrowing day for you, my boy.'

Albert noticed the Sunday-best voice usually reserved for customers and put it down to the newspaper item. 'It was very upsetting,' he admitted.

'But shall I tell you something?' Mr Callendar said. 'I'm glad it was you and not the others. I wouldn't trust them with a naked woman, even if she was dead.'

'They've got no feelings,' Albert agreed.

'That's the point. You've got feelings, Albert. You've got depth. It's the people like us who suffer.'

What's this? Albert was thinking.

'You get away early tonight — have a restful evening.'

'I haven't done me money yet — '

'Never mind that, my boy. Spend the morning with Hetty tomorrow. Or the day after — take a day off if you feel like it. We'll manage somehow. At a time like this when tragedy strikes at one of our good friends, we have to show a little human feeling, don't we?'

'I feel all right now,' Albert said.

Jack Trevor Story

'I mean my old friend Reggie Corby,' Mr Callendar said.

Aye aye, Albert thought.

'This is a great shock to him,' Mr Callendar said.

'I don't know why,' Albert said. 'If you treat a woman like that you should expect it, shouldn't you?' My God! said Treasure, inside his head.

'We all make mistakes,' Mr Callendar told him, fervently. 'We got to be generous, Albert. He's a broken man.'

'You mean he will be if I tell the coroner his wife's last words,' Albert said.

'Yes, Albert, that's the truth. And I know how you feel about it. How we all feel. It's a matter of conscience and I've thought about it very deeply. You see, you've got to think about the living as well as the dead. I ask myself, what good will it do if Reggie loses public support and fails to get elected on to the council?'

'Between ourselves,' Albert said, 'what good will it do if he gets elected — I mean, what's in it for you, Cally?'

Mr Callendar looked at Albert in a stricken way for a moment. Then, cheerfully changing tactics, he said: 'Have a cigar, Albert — I'll tell you about my plans. . . .'

Albert put his feet up on the desk and lit a cigar.

Mr Callendar was not the most adept at turning his dream into words, but he did manage to convey to Albert a picture of the Callendar Emporium which could take shape on the factory site across the street. Mr Callendar had thought about it so much and he saw it so clearly that he had the habit of talking about the problematical future as though it were already a halcyon past.

'In those days all of this area will be a paved shopping centre,' he said. 'Instead of a catalogue we shall have big shop windows and arcades — get the people in the shop.'

'I should've thought you were doing all right now,' Albert said.

'All right, yes. I am very successful. But this business . . .!' He showed his distaste. 'You know what Solly Cowell said to me last night at the cocktail party? He told me the tally business is a furtive business — you know? Like having a stall on the market. We ain't even represented on the local trades council. Oh, it's all right, but it's got no prestige, Albert. These days you got to have prestige. Besides, look at the types I have to employ!'

There was a small silence between them; Mr Callendar then extricated himself.

'You and me want something better, eh? Imagine a big shop — two, three floors. Real classy goods. Why not? Marks and Spencer started with a street stall. Gordon Selfridge used to have a crummy little shop.' He tapped his chest. 'I can do it. Better than Solly Cowell. You got to think big. You got to have vision. Imagine it, Albert, fifty pretty girls in green overalls with Callendar embroidered on their collars.'

'Where do I come into it?' Albert asked.

'What?' Mr Callendar, carried away, had forgotten that Albert did not come into it; but he had to persuade him to forget Mrs Corby's last words.

'I have great plans for you, Albert,' he said, to gain time. 'How old are you?'

'Twenty-four,' Albert told him. Why did people have to keep asking him his age?

'You could be a departmental manager — in charge of ten or twelve girls,' he added, knowing Albert.

'That might be years,' Albert said.

'And in the meantime,' Mr Callendar told him, 'if I can get Reggie's cooperation and secure an option on the site, you can take over here as manager.'

'What are you going to do?'

This was a new bit of the dream and Mr Callendar was making it up as he went along. 'Once I get the option I shall be busy organizing the Callendar Property Trust and Investments Co. Ltd. Have I mentioned this to you before? Its job will be to raise capital for the store — that's easy once you've got the site. Do you know a site like this is worth a hundred thousand pounds as security these days? I won't have time for this place. You can have this office, Albert — this desk. Any questions?'

Jack Trevor Story

'Can I have my name on the door?' Albert asked.

It drew them together; it was something they had in common. However big the dream, however vague and mist-enshrouded the loftier spires of the castle, what they saw were the small bricks of personal aggrandisement; Callendar's name on the shop-girls' collars, Albert's name on the door.

'Of course, Albert. A. Argyle, Manager. And you can have it printed on the next batch of stationery.'

'When do I start?' Albert asked.

'The sooner you give me your assurance that you won't mention what Mrs Corby said, the sooner I can get on to Reggie and make a deal.'

You two bastards! Treasure said in Albert's head.

'Let me sleep on it,' Albert said.

This hesitation was inexplicable to Mr Callendar. Then he remembered something. 'Of course, your money will go up. I'll increase your basic salary and you can take a bonus as a percentage on total sales — a nice steady figure, Albert.'

In the cigar smoke Albert could see a small white face beneath a high bouffant hair style and a pair of brown eyes waiting, cynically. It was Treasure.

'I'd like to think about it,' Albert said.

Mr Callendar looked at him, puzzled. 'Were you having an affair with Mrs Corby?'

'No,' Albert told him. 'But I liked her. I felt sorry for her. I was trying to help her. I wouldn't like to let her down.'

'A hundred pounds cash,' Mr Callendar said.

Albert said: 'There are some things more important than money, Cally.'

When Albert left the office, Mr Callendar sat staring into space for a long time. Albert wouldn't like to let somebody down for a hundred pounds cash? There's your tally-boy! You couldn't even rely on them being unreliable.

He checked the time then rang Chas. Arthur Ltd. Mr Corby was not expected back. Before he could ring his home number the telephone buzzed and Reggie Corby was on the line, angry and threatening.

'Have you talked to your salesman yet?'

'Yes, don't worry, Reggie. He's going to think it over—'

'Well, let him think this over,' Reggie said. 'If he goes blabbing to the police I'm going to ask them to ask him what happened to three pounds my wife had in her handbag — it could look very ugly for him.'

'Hold on a minute, Reggie. That might be useful.' Mr Callendar cupped the receiver and called: 'Albert!'

Arnold put his head in at the door. 'He's just having a slash — anything I can do?'

Albert appeared, pushing Arnold out and closing the door after him.

'Albert — did you take three pounds from Mrs Corby's handbag today?'

'Yes,' Albert said. 'She promised it to me — I thought she'd gone out and forgotten. I've marked it up in her account — you can see the book if you like.'

Mr Callendar motioned him to stand by and spoke again to the telephone: 'Reggie — are you there? Yes, he took it — she had promised it to him. He's marked it up to her account — yes, I realize that, but —'

Albert took the receiver out of Mr Callendar's hand.

'Mr Corby — you tell the police I took the money and I'll tell them where she got it from. Okay?' Albert gave the receiver back to his boss. 'He's not talking.'

'I hope you haven't upset him!' Mr Callendar spoke again to the telephone: 'Reggie? Are you there, Reggie?' He looked at Albert, distraught. 'It sounds as if he's crying!'

Albert shrugged. 'I don't expect he wants everyone to know his wife had to go out to work.'

Mr Callendar's eyes widened with interest. 'Is that what it is? That's useful.' And to the phone. 'Hello, Reggie? Don't worry. Nobody's going to say anything. You stick by me, I'll stick by you. . . . '

Albert sneered as he went out. What a pair. They even made him feel superior.

13

AT the police station the detective superintendent was in conference with the chief constable considering the statements so far received from Albert, Mrs Jenkins, and the dead woman's husband.

'The lady upstairs seems to think she jumped out of the window to get away from him,' the chief constable remarked. 'Is there anything in that, superintendent?'

'I shouldn't think so, sir — not unless she moved the dressing-table to do it.' He laughed. 'Perhaps he helped her?'

The woman police constable was still sitting at the desk, writing. Her pen hesitated for a moment at the laughter, but she did not look up.

'When there's a naked woman involved,' the superintendent said, 'there's always somebody ready with perverted ideas.'

'Do you think it was an accident, then? If she had moved the dressing-table and forgot about it — that would account for it. According to the doctor's report there was soapy water on her face. And a towel on the dressing-table. It looks as though she heard the bell, rushed straight out of the bathroom and through the window — terrible shock for her.'

'Still,' the superintendent said, 'she was dead on impact. Didn't know much about it.'

'On the other hand,' the chief constable said, 'she might have heard the bell, realized it was another creditor, and jumped out of the window. It's happened before — I mean, there have been several suicides. Housewives in debt — all this hire-purchase they seem to go in for.'

'Have to let the coroner sort that one one,' the superintendent said. 'I don't think it was that, somehow — not if she knew who it was. They got on very well.'

'What sort of chap is he — this Argyle?' the chief constable asked. 'Seemed to have great presence of mind — not many people would have had the courage to try mouth-to-mouth respiration.'

'Oh, he's all right. Sid knows him.' The superintenedent shouted: 'Sid! Got a minute?' And when the constable looked in, he said: 'You know Mr Argyle — what's he like?'

'Who, Albert? Oh, he's all right, he is. I knew him at school — when he was there! None of the girls were safe, y'know! Great boy, Albert!'

'Was that grammar school?' the chief constable asked.

'Grammar school?' the superintendent exclaimed, scornfully. 'I should think not! He's a sound lad, he is.'

'One of the boys!' said Sid.

'Thanks, Sid.' The constable went and the superintendent continued: 'Now Corby — he's different. There's your grammar school man. All side! The courts are full of 'em. If it's not fraudulent conversion it's drunk in charge. What? I wouldn't give one house room! And we've had a few on the force — but they never stay. You know why, don't you? Prejudice! They hate the working classes. All prejudice.' He noticed that the chief constable had fallen silent and checked himself: 'Still, that's not pertinent, is it? Let's get back to the facts.'

While they were engaged with the facts, Miss Alcott was shown into the office; she was holding a copy of the evening paper and a small booklet. The chief constable sat aside while the superintendent interviewed her.

'I understand you know something about this case, Miss Alcott — is that right?'

'I don't know whether it has any bearing or not,' Miss Alcott said, 'but it seems to me it might have. Perhaps you remember this booklet? You told me to get in touch with the police and lock myself in the back room if that man ever came in again — well, that's him in the paper!'

'Corby?' the superintendent said.

'No — Mr Argyle. That's the young man who wrote these dreadful poems — not that I knew what they were at the time.'

The superintendent scanned the duplicated book. 'But that was two years ago, Miss Alcott — you can't start bringing charges against him now, y'know.'

'I'm not bringing a charge,' the lady said. 'It was you that wanted him. Don't you remember?'

'Oh, was it? Well, there was a purge on against this kind of thing at the time, I suppose. Harmless stuff, really. Still, thanks for letting me know. You can leave it with us.' He handed the book to the woman police constable. 'File this, will you?'

Miss Alcott was shown out. The woman police constable scanned the contents of the book, blushed, and quickly laid it aside.

'Can I see that?' the chief constable asked.

As he read the obscene poems, the superintendent came and looked over his shoulder. 'Clever stuff in its way, y'know.'

The chief constable looked up at him, stunned: 'What kind of mind invented all this?'

'Oh, I doubt whether he made it up,' the superintendent said. 'He's not the type. Probably got it off lavatory walls — he's one of the boys, he is. Anything for a laugh!'

The woman police constable had not yet been able to resume work when another visitor was announced.

'Another twisted mind,' the superintendent said. 'We're really getting them this time.'

'A Miss Teresa Hunter,' the desk sergeant said.

Treasure came into the room holding the evening paper. Pretty, slim, neatly dressed, and burning with a quiet, angry flame.

'This man is a murderer,' she said. 'And he's not going to get away with it this time!'

'Who's this — Mr Corby?' the superintendent asked.

'Albert Argyle,' Treasure said. 'And that's not even his right name. His real name is Albert Harris. When you've conducted an autopsy you'll find that poor woman was pregnant. That's why he pushed her out of the window.'

'Sit down, will you, miss?' the superintendent asked. 'Now then — how do you know all this?'

'Because he pushed me down two flights of stairs for the same reason!' Treasure said.

The superintendent looked at the girl more closely. 'Haven't I seen you working at the bingo hall?'

'Yes.'

'Ah — I thought so.' He glanced at the chief constable with understanding. 'Very well, miss. We'll look into it.'

'I don't want you to look into it! I want you to arrest him.'

'Well, that's for us to say, miss. Meanwhile I shouldn't go saying things like that — you might get yourself into serious trouble.'

It looked for a moment as though the girl was about to launch herself at the detective. The chief constable intervened, gently.

'I think you should bring Mr Argyle in, superintendent, to answer these charges personally.'

'Do you, sir? It's a bit of an imposition on him, isn't it? I mean, he's had a very harrowing day — ' then at a sudden whitening of Treasure's knuckles on the arm of her chair, he called: 'Dick!' And when a sergeant came in: 'Go down to Callendar's and ask Mr Argyle if he'd mind calling here when it's convenient for him — try not to upset him. Tell him it's nothing very important — '

'You tell him he's a murderer!' Treasure interrupted, rudely. 'And watch him run!'

Over her head the superintendent motioned the sergeant to ignore this direction.

Then he said: 'Would you mind waiting outside, miss? He may be some time.'

When she had gone the superintendent shook his head and sighed. 'Poor devil!' he exclaimed, softly.

The woman police constable looked round at him. 'Who?'

'Him,' said the superintendent. 'Fancy having that round your neck!'

'Good grief!' the woman police constable exclaimed. She got on with her work.

When Albert came out of Callendar's Warehouse a police car was waiting by the kerbside and the sergeant beckoned him over.

'The super would like to see you at the station. I thought it best not to come inside — only cause a lot of talk.'

'What is it, then? I gave him my statement.'

At this moment Albert's attention was taken by something that was happening a little way up the street. Idiot! He had forgotten to put the cover on his car and now a man was trying keys in the lock!

'Some girl came in,' the sergeant said. 'Bit of a nut case if you ask me. There you are, it's never safe to get your face in the papers. It happened to my chum when he won the third dividend — he got stuck with two years back maintenance. Lost the lot!'

The hire-purchase agent was now going back to his own car, having failed to open Albert's door.

'This one's raving,' the sergeant said. 'She reckons you murdered that Corby piece — '

He broke off, for Albert had suddenly dashed away.

'Mr Argyle!' the sergeant called.

But Albert got into his car and drove away.

'That's funny!' the sergeant said.

'Should we follow him?' asked the constable at his side.

'I don't think so. The super didn't say anything about bringing him in. Get on the blower.'

The hire-purchase man had also jumped into his car and was setting off in hot pursuit of Albert.

'Bloody civilians!' the sergeant grumbled. 'Always trying to get the limelight. Hello, super? He's made a run for it!'

'Who's that — Corby?'

'No — Mr Argyle.'

'Oh, that's all right. He'll be back.'

'It's all right,' the sergeant said to the constable.
They drove away.

The town was not designed for a car chase. Through the main street there was a set of traffic lights every fifty yards. At the first of these Albert's pursuer stopped behind him at the red, jumped out his car and ran forward to Albert.

'Mr Argyle — I have a warrant for the re-possession of this — '

The lights changed, Albert went into gear, the hire-purchase man dashed back to his own car and started up again. At the second set of lights the same thing happened.

'Mr Argyle!' the man said, breathlessly, holding Albert's arm through the window. 'I have a warrant for the re-possession — '

Again came the yellow and Albert drove on; the hire-purchase man raced back to his car and got away with hooters blowing behind him. It happened again at the next set of lights, but the time was decreasing.

'Mr Argyle — I have a warrant — '

The lights changed and Albert put his foot down. This time the man was in trouble with the following drivers, several of whom overtook him, swearing, before he could get away. At the next lights the hire-purchase man had more of a run and arrived just as the lights were changing. He managed to get his hand on Albert's arm.

'Mr Argyle!'

'Evening,' Albert said, driving away.

He left the main street and took the road out towards the ring-road. He was now enjoying the chase. Poor sod, he thought. He hasn't a clue. If I did my re-possessions like that I'd expect to lose my job. If that'd been me I'd be sitting on the bonnet now. 'Get off, you stupid clot!' he called, as though it had really happened. Then he glanced into his mirror and found the following car. 'Let's see who's best at geography,' he said.

Albert took the next turning on the right, the first on

Jack Trevor Story

the right again, one on the left, then straight ahead to a T-junction. He had to wait an irritating moment to get on to the main road; in that moment the following car came into view behind him.

'Local man,' Albert said.

He concentrated. He overtook everything he came to, taking chances and getting hooted at. Five minutes later he struck the twin-track ring-road and got up to top speed. He had now lost the pursuing car and he lit a cigarette. Manager, eh? His name on the door? And on the stationery. It would look good. He would be able to pay off all his debts. This car would be his! Not before time — it was bloody nearly worn out.

He came to an island, circled it and travelled back on the opposite track of the same road towards town. Suddenly he saw the hire-purchase man rooting towards him in the opposite direction. Albert eased over to the grass dividing verge, put his finger on the hooter button and kept it there. He glimpsed the poor chap's anguished face as they flashed past each other in opposite directions at a combined hundred-and-twenty miles an hour.

'That's how fast you have to be to catch Alberts,' he said, unfairly taking all the credit.

And then he said: 'Murdered who!' Worried, he drove on. The bitch! She wouldn't! But he knew she would. She still hated him, then? Well, at least it meant that she hadn't grown indifferent.

14

WHEN Albert walked into the reception room at the police station, Treasure sprang to her feet and threw a small brown suitcase at his head.

'You're going to hang!' she said.

The superintendent had witnessed this scene as he came out of his office. 'Would I be right in saying,' he said, 'that the witness is biased?'

Albert was staring down at the floor. The suitcase had broken open and from it had come a shoal of letters.

'Yes, they're all yours,' Treasure told him. 'Summonses, writs, last demands, distraints, do you know I've been sleeping on the floor without a bed for the past two months?' And to the superintendent she added: 'There's even a judgement for ten pounds he owes on his mother's funeral — and she's been dead two years.'

'Not quite two years,' Albert said.

'Is your mother dead?' the superintendent said. 'I'm very sorry.'

Baffled, Treasure stared from Albert to justice. The woman police constable came out on her way home; she gripped the girl's arm in passing. 'You're wasting your time, dear — he's one of the boys.'

'Now let's be fair,' the superintendent said. 'Even if this is just a lovers' tiff — I don't mind listening.'

'She hates me!' Albert said, quickly, at Treasure's swift reaction to this mistake.

With this fact established, she said: 'I advertised for a room-mate — this was nearly two years ago. He turned up!'

'That wasn't an advertisement, darling — that was a message!' Albert said.

'Bad jokes,' she said, 'get worse when they're repeated.'

'You laughed at the time,' Albert told her.

'I didn't know you.'

'We were together eighteen months,' Albert told the superintendent, mistily.

'One month getting to know you,' Treasure said, 'the other seventeen trying to get my own back!'

'You weren't happy together?' the superintendent hazarded.

'I was happy!' said Albert.

'And why not?' Treasure said. 'Eating my food, using my furniture, my gas, electricity!'

'Sleeping in your bed,' Albert reminded her, gently.

'And when I got pregnant he pushed me downstairs!'

'It was your suggestion,' Albert told her.

'All I said was it happened to a friend of mine — and that was a pure accident!'

'Well there you are then,' Albert said. 'I knew it wouldn't work if you were expecting it.'

'It didn't work anyway,' she said.

'What happened?' the superintendent asked.

'I was on crutches for a fortnight!' Treasure said.

'I mean about the baby?' asked the detective.

'I lost him when we were at the pictures one night,' Treasure said. 'Just when I didn't want to lose him.'

'Him!' Albert exclaimed.

'A woman knows,' Treasure said. She looked at the superintendent. 'I was half dead with pain and misery and he said "let's celebrate!" I shall never forgive him for that.'

'I thought that's what it was,' Albert said.

'You're still very sensitive, I see!'

The superintendent said: 'It might have been worse, miss. Supposing you had had the baby? I mean, if you hate him so much — you might have been married to him now.'

'Marry!' Treasure exclaimed. 'Albert marry? He would only marry himself!' Then she said, 'Besides, I wouldn't have hated him if I'd had the baby.'

'You wanted my baby?' Albert said, softly.

'Well, let's face it,' she said, 'you never gave my anything else in the whole time we were together!'

'They were difficult times,' Albert said. 'I was missing my mother.'

'You mean I failed you?' Treasure said. 'I can't think in what tiny way. Of course, I wasn't quite as soft as your mother — I didn't work myself to death.'

'That's unkind,' the superintendent said.

'I feel unkind,' Treasure told him. 'I want you to hang him. Even apart from this latest murder he deserves it — he killed his mother, he killed his son, he almost killed me — and I can't think of one exonerating circumstance except that he's Albert. Is there a separate law for the Alberts of this world?'

'She doesn't mean it,' Albert told the superintendent. 'It's just her extravagant way of talking.' He looked at Treasure. 'I don't hate you, Treasure.'

'Try to think of one reason why you should!'

'You came down to Callendar's and broke the place up — I'm still paying for that.'

'Are you?' she said. 'Well, that's a comfort — I wish I'd known.' And to the detective she explained: 'You can only hurt Albert if you hit him in his pocket.'

'I'm afraid a lot of us are like that these days, miss,' the superintendent told her.

The girl looked at the detective superintendent in sudden weariness. 'You're not going to believe that Albert killed this woman, are you?'

'I know he didn't,' the superintendent said.

'You believe he was in a flat with a naked woman and that was a coincidence?' Treasure said.

'I was not in the flat,' Albert said. 'I was ringing the doorbell when she fell. I thought I heard her scream and I went in. At first I didn't know where she was. Then I heard somebody calling and I looked out of the window. I saw this woman upstairs — and then I saw Mrs Corby under the window. Do you believe me?'

'Yes, of course,' said the detective.

'Do you?' Albert was talking to Treasure and looking her straight in the eye.

She refused to admit that she believed him; instead she said: 'Why were you ringing the doorbell?'

'I was collecting,' Albert said.

'That's his job,' the superintendent said.

'Why were you there?' Treasure said.

'I told you — '

'That's not the truth, Albert.'

'Look, miss,' the detective said, 'if it's his job to — '

'No, it's not the truth,' Albert admitted, wearily. 'I was hoping to make her — it was as good as in the bag.'

'That's better,' Treasure said.

'It's not really pertinent,' the superintendent said.

'Her husband might think so,' Treasure said.

'Are you trying to make trouble for me?' Albert asked her.

'Yes. If I can't see you hanged I'd like to see you beaten up. Just once would do.'

Albert said: 'You're going to hurt Mr Corby more than you hurt me, Treasure.'

'He's right,' the superintendent said.

Treasure looked to heaven. 'You see what I mean?' she said. She went out of the police station, walking over the debris of Albert's old bills.

Albert and the detective superintendent looked at each other for a moment.

'Phew — mate,' said the superintendent.

Albert gave him a brave smile before scooping the documents into the case and leaving.

Albert hurried out of the police station, clutching the unfastened case and searching for Treasure. She was about to step off the pavement and cross the road when he spotted her.

'Treasure! Treasure, don't go!'

She did not even turn her head. She had heard him, Albert knew that; it was just that it diminished a man to have to run. Albert ran, catching up with her as she reached the far side of the road. He fell into step with her.

'Can I give you a lift?'

Treasure just kept walking. She had a nice, easy stride; she had nice long legs, it reminded him, if he needed any reminder. Sideview, from his height, her face gave the impression that she had forgotten him; that she was not unaware of his presence, but slightly irritated that some stranger should be presuming an acquaintance.

'Come on, Treasure,' he said, 'I know you're there.'

Caught unaware her lips quivered like a ventriloquist trying to prevent mouth movement.

'That's better. No hard feelings, eh?' She quickened her pace and he skipped to get into step. 'What do you think of the political situation in Transcaucasia?' he asked. She stopped walking suddenly and he made a pretence of over-shooting, then shunted back to her like an engine. 'You should have an air-brakes warning on your back!'

She had waited long enough for him to see that she was not amused, then said: 'I don't know where you're going, but I'm going home.'

'That's funny,' he said. 'You used to know where I was going.'

'I don't even think you're funny any more.'

'Well, it's an old picture — stick around, I've got new stuff.'

'You are annoying me,' she said.

'Annoying you! But darling, don't you see? This is a fantastic improvement — you used to hate my guts!'

'You haven't got any guts.'

Albert laughed, delightedly. 'Now who's being nostalgic?'

'You are a self-centred, ego-maniacal crumb!'

'These foolish things remind me of you, too,' Albert said. 'Remember? The night I sleep-walked and you opened the window? The lighted cigarette you put in my shoe? Those hours I spent nailed in the lavatory? Don't they mean anything to you?'

'Get out of my way,' Treasure said. 'I don't want to know you.'

'Now you know it's too late for that, darling.' She was walking and he fell into step with her again. 'That's what I really miss. Nobody knows me the way you know me.'

'Don't bank on it,' she said. 'I'm hoping there's a God.'

'You can say that? You just tried to get me hanged!'

'That was just a silly, wishful impulse,' she said.

And then all at once she laughed; but bit it off, quickly.

'Oh my God,' Albert said. 'You haven't changed, have you — you still only laugh at your own jokes.'

'Then why bother?'

'Shall I tell you? It's because you're my only failure. Everybody else I've fooled. After all we went through together — '

'After all *I* went through together.'

'After all you went through together I don't like being strangers. I miss you, Treasure. I want to make it up to you.'

'You want to take me to bed tonight.'

'I want to take you to bed tonight — ' he pretended to remember himself. 'I mean . . . '

'You decided to try and take me to bed from the moment I threw that case at you in the police station,' she told him.

'You see? I knew you were only flirting!' Albert said. He offered the case. 'Here, do it again!'

'You'll never make love to me again,' Treasure said.

'Oh yes I will!'

'Oh no you won't!'

'Oh yes I will — and I won't use a contraceptive!'

'Oh yes you will!' she said.

They both laughed. They had stopped on a street corner. It was growing dark, the street lights were on.

'You see?' Albert said. 'We still laugh at the old jokes.'

She looked at him, soberly. 'You always thought a laugh took the place of everything. It doesn't, Albert. You think I haven't changed, but I have. Being a mother changed me — but you don't even know you were a father. That's something you're too selfish to know. You're a tally-boy. A wife to you is a bit of crumpet. You've got no respect for other people's marriages and you'd have none for your own.'

'I respect you, Treasure,' Albert said.

'Well,' she said, 'you did wait until I'd gone into hospital to get over my miscarriage before walking out on me — I suppose that's a kind of respect.'

Albert said: 'I didn't walk out on you — I walked out on the post man and the bailiff and the police. Everybody was catching up on me at once. I couldn't leave an address. I meant to come and see you — then you came down to the shop. Well, I didn't think it was any use, then. But I've felt worse about it every time I've thought about it. I've started talking to you when I'm alone. I mean it.'

Treasure stared at him. 'This is new,' she said. 'I should have to have time to figure this one out.'

'I miss you like hell,' he said.

'No,' she said. 'It's not that.'

'You're like a conscience — I told Grace that this morning. You see, I was talking about you this morning.'

She said: 'How's your eldest? The youngest is dead.'

'Isn't that a bond between us?' Albert said, earnestly.

'No,' she said. 'Not a bond, Albert. Whatever the opposite of a bond is, that's what's between us.'

'A gulf?'

'That'll do,' she said.

'Well, what do you think it is? My talking to you when I'm alone, I mean?'

'Well, I don't know. But I suppose the feeling of being with somebody who knows what a swine you are could give you a sense of peace or something.'

'I think that's it,' Albert said. 'That's what I miss. When I'm with you I don't have to put on an act or make conversation — '

'Or be civil or polite or thoughtful, or spend money,' she added.

Albert laughed. 'Look, while we're chatting here I could be driving you home. Just to the door. I wouldn't get out of the car. And you can sit on the back seat — by yourself, I mean — as we're going. It's no trouble, Treasure. It'd be a privilege.'

'Are you trying to tell me you've changed, Albert?'

'No. We never change, darling — but you can feel worse about the way you are.'

It took her by surprise and she stared at him again, as though for something missed. 'Did you read that in a book? But I forgot, you don't read books.'

'I thought about it when I found that girl dead this afternoon. She was a good type — a real sweetie. I felt awful, Treasure. I was sick.'

'Death does something to you,' Treasure said. Then she said: 'All right, Albert — you can drive me home.'

He took hold of her arm and looked at her, tenderly:

'Do you still hate me?'

'Yes — I shall always hate you,' she said, softly.

'Even when I'm old and grey?'

'Even more then,' she said.

She took his hand off her arm and they walked back separate and apart, but also together.

They came back towards the police station, chatting like old friends.

'You haven't ridden in the new car yet, have you?' Albert said.

'No, but I've had all the demand notes. They've been trying to find it for weeks. Quite a nice man — he put up some bookshelves for me.'

'Well that's all taken care of now — Cally's making me manager. Did I tell you? More money, a bonus, no more tallying — '

'You're talking to me — did you forget?'

'It's true, Treasure!'

'Then you must have got something on him at last.'

'In a way, yes.' He told her about Reggie Corby and Callendar's anxiety to make a property deal. 'He's worried sick I'll bring it out at the inquest.'

'But you'll have to — why should he get away with it if he drove her to suicide?'

'But didn't I tell you? She didn't say it. I made it up. You know how I make things up. She was dead when I found her — how could she say anything? But I knew what he was afraid of when he asked me. "Have you told the police?" he said. Why, he made her life a misery.'

'So you're going to cash in on it?'

'I didn't say I would. I said I might.'

'You said he was going to make you manager.'

'Well, I don't see why not. I mean, I'm not lying or breaking the law if I forget something that was never said — it's just his bad conscience that's paying dividends.'

'It's also blackmail,' Treasure said.

'How is it blackmail? I didn't go to them — they came to me. I wouldn't even have thought of saying what she said if he hadn't asked me. Besides, it's time I got a responsible job and more money. I've earned it. I've pushed the sales higher than anybody he's ever had.'

'You'll never settle in an office,' Treasure told him. 'You're a tally-boy. It's not just a job, it's a state of mind. Wayward, irresponsible, fly-by-night, immoral — you've got all the qualifications, Albert.'

'Not me, darling. Not any more. You're talking about Jeff and Arnold. I want something with a bit of prestige to it. These days you've got to have prestige.'

'Are you still giving Marjorie her weekly tumble?' Treasure asked, politely.

'What a disgusting thing to say! You've never met her husband. I like Cedric. He talks a lot of cock but I respect him. After all, he was my schoolmaster.'

'That means you are,' Treasure said. 'You'd never settle in a humdrum office, even if it did have your name on the door.'

Albert made no reply to this; he knew she was there even while Callendar was making the offer. They came to the car and the hire-purchase man was sitting behind the wheel.

'Hello, Mr Drake!' Treasure said. 'You've caught up with him, then?'

'Good evening, Miss Hunter.' And then to Albert: 'I think you know the rules, sir. When we've sold the car you'll be held responsible for the liability.'

'You know the big end's gone, do you?' Albert said. 'I just came back to cover it up for the night — the garage were collecting it in the morning.'

'The big end?' Mr Drake said. 'That's an eighty pound job on this model!'

'I know,' Albert told him. 'You'll have to have it seen to before you sell it. Oh, and it's not insured for any other driver — you'll need special cover before you can take it away, anyway.'

'My insurance covers that,' Mr Drake said.

'Oh. Well, just the big end, then.'

'Of course,' Mr Drake said, 'if you brought your payments up to date now you could keep it.'

'It's hardly worth it, really,' Albert said. 'How much do I owe in arrears?'

'Fifty pounds,' Mr Drake said. 'I shouldn't really accept it at this late stage, but in view of what you've told me . . . '

'Okay — jump out,' Albert said.

He took the wad of notes from his inside pocket and nonchalantly counted them. Treasure and Mr Drake watched. Only Drake was impressed.

'There you are, old man.' Albert gave the notes to Mr Drake, who carefully recounted them before making out a receipt.

Mr Drake was half-way back to his own car when he heard Albert start up. Looking rather sick he watched the car move smoothly away.

15

'THAT was Callendar's money,' Treasure said, as Albert drove her across town.

'I can make my own terms with Cally in the morning.'

'You're getting a power complex,' Treasure told him.

Albert grinned at her; the little brush with the hire-purchase man and having Treasure there made him feel suddenly in command. And he knew that he could get Treasure home to bed. He was not certain where this was going to lead, but it was what he wanted now. But she would need a drink or two; Treasure had always got help-less on cider.

'How would you like to come to a party?' he asked her.

'You're driving me home,' she reminded him. Don't do it, the inner voice told her. You shouldn't even be in the car. You shouldn't have dawdled when you came out of the police station.

'All right — just as you like. I shan't go. I'm not very

Live Now, Pay Later   131

keen on parties these days. Don't know many people.'

'Why do you say things like that to me?' she said. 'This car stinks of cheap scent.'

'Well, I've been out with one or two girls,' he admitted. 'But they bore me to death — talk talk talk!'

'I talk talk talk,' Treasure said.

'That's different,' he said. 'You talk about me.'

She laughed spontaneously. 'What sort of party?' she asked.

'A jazz party in Beachfield Road — a rock group and so on. I suppose there'll be some food. They wanted me to get along to ginger things up if I could. But I don't know, I suppose it'll be crowded with kids.'

'You mean you know where there's a party going on which you might be able to gatecrash,' Treasure said.

'That's right.'

They drove on in silence for a minute, then she said: 'I've got nothing to wear, anyway. Not for parties.'

'I can soon fix that!' Albert said.

He took the next turning towards Callendar's Warehouse. Stop him! Treasure's inner voice exclaimed. She wasn't listening.

The women's clothing department at Callendar's Warehouse was well stocked with mass-produced model dresses in the enormous range of fittings necessary for an off-the-peg business.

'Does Mr Callendar know you've got a key?' Treasure asked.

She was holding a pretty green sleeveless number up to herself and judging its effect in a long mirror.

'Not yet,' Albert said. 'But it'll soon be official — '

'Keep your hands off me!' Treasure said.

Albert had been draping the dress around her hips; he now stood back, obediently.

Treasure looked at him in the mirror: 'No obligation, you know — I'm just borrowing it.'

'No obligation, madam,' Albert confirmed.

He left her to browse amongst the dresses and petti-

Jack Trevor Story

coats and lingerie and went himself to the men's wear department. She heard him singing and her heart sang too; in a big warehouse filled with gay modern styles they felt like children in a toy factory with no one to supervise them. She chose shoes, stockings, panties, bra, petticoat, and a bright crimson dress.

'Albert!' she called.

Don't do it, said the voice.

'I'm not doing anything!' she replied.

Albert came through a curtain of coats dressed in a dinner-jacket suit with bow-tie and black suede shoes.

'You look marvellous!' he said.

'So do you!' she told him. Then, dubiously, 'Shall we be all right for a jazz party?'

'Will they be all right for us?' Albert said.

'You're having them all back,' Treasure told him at the look in his eye.

'On the stroke of midnight!'

'I don't know about that.'

'Come on,' Albert said. 'Let's see what happens.'

'Just keep your hands off me,' she said.

He tucked his hands inside the breast of his jacket and followed her out with a comic, cringing walk.

She felt him close behind her and shivered in the old way. 'Don't put the lights out till I'm outside!' she said.

They found the party in Beachfield Road by the number of scooters and motor-cycles parked outside. It was a semi-detached house full of teenagers and parents away. The lights were low, the hall, stairs, passages were clogged with motionless snogging shapes. Three young men were wedged into the front bay window playing an electric guitar, drums and bass. Four or five couples jived desperately in the middle of the room. Albert burst straight in:

'Carry on, folks!' he exclaimed. 'As if I were just an ordinary person!'

'Who the hell are you, then?' asked a literal-minded boy in charge of drinks by the door.

'Friend of Peter's,' Albert said. 'Peter Barnwell — he's here, isn't he?'

'Bloody cheek!' the boy said. Then he called: 'Pete!'

Peter laid aside his guitar and came over.

'This chap says he knows you. You might ask before inviting people!'

Peter stared hard at Albert, then at Treasure. 'I don't know you!'

'Either you know me,' Albert said, 'or I'm taking that guitar back!'

'I know him,' Peter said. 'Anyway, we can do with more girls.' He took Treasure's hand. 'You come upstairs; I'll show you where to put your coat — you can look after the drinks,' he said to Albert.

'Here, just a minute!' Albert said, as Treasure allowed herself to be led away.

'Share and share alike, mate — we're always short on birds,' the other boy said. 'Haven't bought any drink, have you?'

'Whose party is this?' Albert asked. 'Yours or mine?'

Without the uncertain melody of the guitar the drums and bass went on producing a thumping rhythm. Albert poured himself half a tumbler of whisky.

'Any vintage cider?' he asked the boy.

During the next two hours Albert and Treasure caught sight of each other through the crowd now and then; she stepped over him snogging on the stairs, he stepped over her similarly engaged.

'How about a dance?' Albert had pulled a young man's head aside to ask her the question.

'Don't do it!' she said. Then she hiccuped. 'I wasn't supposed to say that — sorry. Not on top of that cider — where's it keep coming from?'

'There's another glass just by your hand,' Albert said, passing on.

By midnight Albert had run his technique over every girl in the house, drunk half a bottle of whisky, jived, played the drums and was now raiding the kitchen.

'Albert!'

Jack Trevor Story

He stopped cutting cheese to listen, his mouth full. Treasure's voice came distantly above the sound of the music, talking, and dancing. It didn't come again and he went on listening for a moment. He popped another piece of cheese into the mouth of a girl sitting on the table.

'Have you ever kissed while you're eating?' she asked.

'You kids!' Albert said. 'Always looking for some perversion!'

He stopped kissing her and listened again. 'Stay there!' he said. 'Don't move. . . . '

He went slowly out of the kitchen and through the dark passage, stepping over shapes. The trouble was, in his head she was always calling him.

'You can't go up there, mate — they're busy!' A large youth blocked his way on the stairs.

Albert hooked his arm around the youth's neck and yanked him down the stairs. He went to the only bedroom with a closed door, burst in. In the half-darkness he found two youths holding Treasure on the bed; all he could see of her was her bare legs. Albert swung them off one at a time, crashing his big fist into their faces. Treasure scrambled off the bed, pulling her clothes together.

'Get out to the car!' Albert told her.

She rushed out of the room and down the stairs, through the hall and out of the front door, up the garden path and into the car, slamming the door behind her. She was sitting in the front seat, her head on her lap, crying, when Albert came out.

'I've got the guitar,' he said. He put it on the back seat, started the motor and drove away. 'Have they mucked that dress up?' he asked.

Treasure's crying turned into hysterical laughter. With one hand on the wheel he turned and slapped her face, hard. She slapped his, harder.

'You're not supposed to do that!' Albert said.

'You bastard!' she said. 'You nearly had me fooled again!'

Albert looked at her. 'I don't get it! I did my best! I should've thought you might have thanked me!'

'What for?' Treasure said.

He stared at her in astonished disbelief that slowly turned to appalled belief. She lowered her head and covered her face with her hands.

'I'll kill them!' he muttered.

'Just take me home,' she said. 'And don't get out of the car. . . . '

'Mr Callendar wants to see you, Mr Argyle,' Hetty said as Albert came in the next morning.

Jeff and Arnold were sorting the day's merchandise.

'What've you been up to, old chappie?' Jeff asked.

'You want to watch yourself,' Albert told him. 'There's going to be a few changes around here.'

'So I understand,' Jeff said.

Albert looked from smirking face to smirking face.

'You want to clear up after yourself when you bring birds in at night,' Arnold said. 'I always do.'

Puzzled, Albert tapped the office door and entered. Mr Callendar did not immediately look up from his paperwork; this was a depressing sign.

'I've decided not to say anything,' Albert said, kicking off on an optimistic note.

Mr Callendar looked at him. 'That's very good of you, Albert — considering she was dead on hitting the ground.'

'She couldn't have been!'

'Two doctors say so — I wouldn't go against them if I were you.'

'I didn't actually tell the police,' Albert said.

'Now we know why, don't we? Mr Corby is not very pleased.'

'What's he doing about the site?'

'This is not your business, Albert. Sit down. I want you to explain one or two things. . . . '

It was one of Mr Callendar's specific criticisms and this time he had a lot to go on. A pair of girl's panties found in the showroom, signs of clothes having been taken — though what kind and now many Hetty's book-keeping had failed to reveal. The washing-machine returned from

Mrs Mason had never been purchased at Callendar's at all — it was the wrong make and five years old.

'I also took the liberty of going through the suit you left here last night — since you had taken the liberty of wearing one of ours. Your accounts book shows fifty pounds collected yesterday — '

'You told me not to bother to pay it in until this morning,' Albert reminded him.

'So I did,' Mr Callendar agreed. 'Give it to me now.'

'Now?'

'Now,' Mr Callendar said.

'Okay — I'll give it to Hetty.'

'I asked you to give it to me,' Mr Callendar said.

'Don't you trust me or something?'

Mr Callendar picked up a slip of paper which he had also found in Albert's suit pocket. Albert stared at it; it was the receipt for fifty pounds from the hire-purchase man.

'Well, what else could I do?' Albert said. 'I'll pay you back — you know that.'

'That's the only reason I'm not ringing the police.' Mr Callendar said. 'You remember what happened to Max? I'm going to be lenient with you this time, Albert.'

'Stop it out of my money,' Albert said.

'I will — but don't depend on Hetty's book-keeping this time. I shall keep a separate account. With the damage your girl-friend did you owe me a hundred pounds, not counting what you took from here when you broke in last night.'

'I didn't break in — I've got a key! Yesterday I was going to be manager!'

'If that was your first night's work as manager I can only thank my lucky stars you lost the job — we'll say four pounds a week deducted from your salary, that makes — '

'I can't live on eight quid a week!' Albert exclaimed.

'You'll have to step up your sales, won't you — one more thing. What's this?'

Mr Callendar was holding the petition for the tree

which he had also found in Albert's pocket. Albert explained what it was. Mr Callendar expressed his incredulity.

'You're helping the old folk save their tree and getting nothing in return?'

'You've got to help people sometimes,' Albert said.

'If you're going to start being eccentric, don't do it in my time, please, Albert.'

'We're all doing it!' Albert said. 'Why pick on me?'

'It's incredible!' Mr Callendar said. 'Loaded atom bombs all over the world, the Common Market only two steps away — and all these people signing a petition to save an old tree!'

'There's a lot of feeling in the town,' Albert said, righteously. 'Somebody's got to stick up for these old people!'

Mr Callendar suddenly had goose-pimples, but they didn't show. 'Get me those other petitions,' he said.

When the tally-boys had gone on their rounds Mr Callendar telephoned Reginald Corby at the Chas. Arthur offices.

'Reggie — have you parted with that option yet? Good — don't do it. I've got something to put you on the council without fail — better than dogs, better than the swimming pool or playing fields. Something the whole town will support you on — I've already got seven hundred and twenty-three bona-fide signatures. Seven hundred and twenty-four,' he said, as he added his own.

When Coral Wentworth answered the door Albert stood there with all her parcels piled high in his arms.

'Father Christmas!' he said. 'Sorry I'm late delivering them, madam!'

'Well I don't know what to say!' she exclaimed. 'I'm afraid you'll have to take them back. My husband's gone on short time — at least, they're working to rule, that's the same thing. I can't honestly afford thirty-three shillings a week now — I'm terribly sorry.'

Jack Trevor Story

'It won't last forever, will it?'

'It might be weeks — they haven't got much consideration for us housewives.'

'Husbands are a dead loss,' Albert said. 'I could've told you that.'

She laughed. 'It's a bit late telling me now!'

'Let's talk about it inside,' Albert suggested. 'I dare say we can manage something between us, darling.'

Coral giggled. 'I don't like the sound of that!' And as she let him in and closed the door: 'You'll have to excuse me — I'm afraid I'm in the middle of dressing.'

Albert followed her through to the sitting-room, appraising her figure wrapped in a flimsy housecoat. He was glad he hadn't swapped her for those girls of Jeff's. Single girls placed too much importance on it. No sense of values.

He helped her unpack the nylon-fur rug, the curb and curb-set, a chiming clock, a parcel of clothes and shoes, a bedside lamp.

'Where does this go?' he asked, holding the lamp.

'As if you didn't know!' Coral said. 'Hasn't Marjorie got one?'

'Oh yes — I remember.'

He followed her upstairs, waiting while she drew the curtains on the landing. He looked at his watch.

Albert was going to be late again.

Other Titles from SAVOY BOOKS

KISS
by Robert Duncan.
(125mm x 193mm)

Rock's arcane heavies give the low down
on the band who rose out of Brooklyn
to stamp a new style of heavy rock'n'roll
on a world gone soft at the poles.
Illustrated.

£1.25 Paperback
ISBN 0 86130 040 8

SCREWRAPE LETTUCE
by Jack Trevor Story.
(125mm x 193mm)

Number seven in Savoy's series of Jack
Trevor Story novels. "The book is
volatile, grotesque, brilliantly messy —
like watching a diamond burst in the
hands" — The Sunday Times. Illustrated.

£1.50 Paperback
ISBN 0 86130 038 6

*

I AM THE GREATEST SAYS JOHNNY ANGELO
by Nik Cohn.
(125mm x 193mm)

Simply the best rock'n'roll fantasy novel ever written.

£1.50 Paperback ISBN 0 86130 041 6

*

MY EXPERIENCES IN THE THIRD WORLD WAR
by Michael Moorcock.
(125mm x 193mm)

A new novel by England's finest living fantasist.

£1.50 Paperback ISBN 0 86130 037 8

*

MUMBO JUMBO
by Ishmael Reed
(125mm x 193mm)

"Part vision, part satire, part farce . . . A wholly original, unholy cross between the craft of fiction and witchcraft" — The New York Times. "A 'HooDoo' thriller, an all-out assault on Western Civilisation . . . Reed's best novel" — Saturday Review. Illustrated

£1.50 Paperback ISBN 0 86130 042 4

*

JAMES DEAN: THE MUTANT KING
by David Dalton
(125mm x 193mm)

A haunting psychological study. David Dalton has found the perfect words to preserve Dean's contribution to the 50's for posterity. An immensely important work. Illustrated

£1.95 Paperback ISBN 0 86130 043 2

*

**THE CRYSTAL AND THE AMULET/
THE SWORD AND THE RUNESTAFF**
Two new collaborations by Michael Moorcock and James Cawthorn
(335mm x 244mm)

"Superior editions of powerful black and white fantasy artwork. Far above the level of comparable American collections in this particular genre of pictorial fiction. Their nearest equivalents are the books of Burne Hogarth" — Newsweek.

£3.50 Paperback ISBN 0 86130 044 0   ISBN 0 86130 045 9

Jack Trevor Story from Savoy Books

LIVE NOW, PAY LATER
(193mm x 125mm)

In the first book of the famous Albert Argyle trilogy the ace conman of the sixties and prince Tally-boy of Jack Trevor Story's provincial town catches the housewives and the reader fast in the grip of Hire Purchase, devious politics and easy payments. 144pp

£1.25 Paperback ISBN 0 86130 029 7
£4.95 Hard Case ISBN 0 86130 030 0

SOMETHING FOR NOTHING
(193mm x 125mm)

The market seems to be dropping out of Hire Purchase and so Albert Argyle switches to Trading Stamps. Never without a woman, superbly, raffishly, entertainingly ruthless. But you can't get something for nothing. 176pp

£1.25 Paperback ISBN 0 86130 031 9
£4.95 Hard Case ISBN 0 86130 032 7

THE URBAN DISTRICT LOVER
(193mm x 125mm)

Jack Trevor Story takes his character to meet his maker in a hilarious, incisive last book written with superb observation, sympathy and wit. 192pp

£1.25 Paperback ISBN 0 86130 033 5
£4.95 Hard Case ISBN 0 86130 034 3